CAPRA BACK-TO-BACK SERIES

1. URSULA K. LE GUIN, The Visionary, *and*
   SCOTT R. SANDERS, Wonders Hidden

2. ANAIS NIN, The White Blackbird *and*
   KANOKO OKAMOTO, The Tale of an Old Geisha

3. JAMES D. HOUSTON, One Can Think About Life
   After the Fish Is In The Canoe *and*
   JEANNE WAKATSUKI HOUSTON, Beyond Manzanar

4. HERBERT GOLD, Stories of Misbegotten Love *and*
   DON ASHER, Angel On My Shoulder

5. RAYMOND CARVER and TESS GALLAGHER
   Dostoyevsky (The Screenplay) *and*
   URSULA K. LE GUIN, King Dog (A Screenplay)

6. EDWARD HOAGLAND, City Tales *and*
   GRETEL EHRLICH, Wyoming Stories

252

HERBERT GOLD

Stories of Misbegotten Love

CAPRA PRESS
1985

ACKNOWLEDGEMENTS

"His Wife and Her Husband," "A Dark Norwegian Person," and "Bart and
Helene at Annie and Fred's" were first published in *Playgirl*.
"San Francisco Petal" appeared in *Playboy*. "Stages" appeared in *Tri-Quarterly*.

Cover design by Francine Rudesill
Design by Jim Cook
Typography by Cook/Sundstrom Associates

Gratitude to the National Endowment for the Arts
for their valuable assistance.

LIBRARY OF CONGRESS CATALOGING IN PUBLICATION DATA
Gold, Herbert, 1924-
STORIES OF MISBEGOTTEN LOVE.
No collective t.p. Titles transcribed from individual title pages.
Texts bound together back to back and inverted.
I. Asher, Don, 1926-   . Angel on my shoulder 1985.
II. Title.   III. Title: Angel on my shoulder.
PS3557.O34S7   1985   813'.54   85-7756
ISBN 0-88496-234-2 (pbk.)

PUBLISHED BY
CAPRA PRESS
Post Office Box 2068
Santa Barbara, Ca. 93120

CONTENTS

1. His Wife & Her Husband / 7
2. Stages / *17*
3. San Francisco Petal / *36*
4. A Dark Norwegian Person / *48*
5. Bart and Helene at Annie and Fred's / *64*

HIS WIFE & HER HUSBAND

SINCE HIS former wife was busy leaving her new husband, and this occasion remains difficult even if a person has been through it before, the least he could do would be to get their daughter out of her hair. He arranged to keep her for the week. By telephone she said, in that calm and friendly way of hers, both alert and preoccupied, "That would be a help, dear."

'Out of her hair'—her lovely rich tumble of mahogany tones now absorbing on a few refractions of gray. For her new marriage she had cut it stylishly short, still surprising him every time he saw her. What he remembered was an abandoned shimmer.

The house looked unsettled as he drove up. It seemed to tilt in the white winter sunlight. Once it had been his, theirs, *ours,* and he remembered how it tilted during their final fights, his final rushing away, and even the furniture seemed to be a jumble when he came hurtling back with one more thing to say, or book to throw, or a plate to break. And then years of calm new routines.

7

And now, as he entered, the house was humming, really humming—some sort of machine at work upstairs.

"Thanks, it's not a good time. I appreciate," she said. She
leaned, he leaned, they pecked. Her skin still smelled like all the
flowers he loved.

"Well. Well. I know," he said. "Where's Dana?"

"She's outside. Must not have heard you drive up. Maybe she's
sitting in the back yard with her hands over her ears."

"Poor kid."

"Nobody gets used to it. And oh, I should tell you—*he's* still
here."

"What?"

"Sprained his back. Lower back, the painfullest part—he
assures me of that. He's in bed, and it hurts to move. Valium and
percodan on the hour."

He was thinking, Did she pinch his vertebrae for him? And
she seemed to hear the thought, because she added: "Lower back is
always often partly psychic, or what I mean, psychological."

"Psychic isn't bad," he said. "Do you have any pains?"

She turned away. "Percodan's not my remedy of choice. It
never gets easier." Then made a milk observation on the weather:
"If it makes you feel any better, I didn't seem to treat Us as a
proper learning experience, did I? Consider this an apology."

"Consider this a don't-worry-about-it."

She flashed her hilarious smile at him, that smile of pure
process, the smile of just in the soup, in the deal, her just doing it
smile—the smile that confirmed him when he fell in love with
her, telling him this woman and her power was the woman for

him. He knew what the joke was—how he managed to turn Fred's spine, her trouble, into their marriage again. "His back'll be okay after awhile. It goes out on him, but then it straightens up, sort of. He was supposed to leave today. He'll stay in our room, his room, and I'll sleep on the couch."

"That's a switch," he said.

"You always said it wasn't too uncomfortable," she said.

They both heard their daughter at the same time. "Dad! I'm up here!"

He called upstairs, "Okay, come on down."

"I'm packing. Come on up and see."

"She cleaned her closets," his former wife said, "and that's a miracle she wants to share with you."

He waited.

His former wife shrugged. This meant, Help yourself. So he trotted upstairs, and realized too late that he would pass their bedroom, and the door was open and his successor was lying there with the cord of a heating pad stretching like a thin tail from beneath the covers. It would only be polite to pause. "Hi, Fred," he said.

"Hi. Howya doing?"

He paused. Would it be correct to say, Sorry about your back? "Sorry about your back," he said.

Fred shrugged from his suffering stiff stretched-out position. He didn't think Fred should by lying on his back, but he was. His face was dark and blotched. His big belly could be seen, or perhaps only imagined, under the layers of bedclothes and quilt. He thought he remembered the quilt—their quilt—but then he

realized it was a new and identical one; she had given the old one
to Goodwill, along with their stainless steel silverware, explaining
that it was mangled by the dishwasher and use and, besides, a new
wife liked to start anew in her flatware with a new husband.

"Well, I guess I better get the kid packed."

Fred waved him on with the kind of shrug a man can make
when down on his back.

He found their daughter looking at a scrapbook, not packing,
her sweaters and books and precious gems piled around her. He
wasn't going to go through that album again; not now, not here.
She had a delicate thickening taking place beneath her cashmere
sweater—it was one of her mother's, washed by mistake and
shrunken—that heart-breaking change in a girl's body; that is, it
broke the heart until he looked at the gum-chewing jaws above,
and then it was just his daughter again. "When you get packed,"
he said, "I'll see you downstairs. But the closet does look nice and
clean. I never saw the light on before."

"Fred fixed up a light for me," she said. "He never told me it
would make me appreciate cleaning it, but it does. That was before
he hurt his back. He didn't do it on my closet, Dad. It got hurt all
by itself."

So he went downstairs to wait for Dana. It was slow work,
packing a ski bag case while looking at an album of photographs
and souvenirs. At twelve years of age, with so much moving so
fast, Dana liked to take her time about things.

He thought about the flushed, blotched, pouting face of the
man with back pains upstairs in his bed, and he remembered the
firm mattress of that bed, thinking it was the firmist and best bed

he had slept in over a long term. But a good-posture mattress
didn't spare Fred his pains. Probably Fred shouldn't have let
himself develop that weight around the middle, adding this strain
to all the other strains. It was not his place to give Fred advice in
the matter.

"She stalling?" his former wife asked.

He ignored the question. "Fred looks kind of gloomy all by
himself up there."

"That's his problem," she said.

"Poor Fred."

She looked at him quizzically. "Are you forming alliances now?
You used to be jealous. I'm sorry for him, but I can't do anymore.
I'll feed him while he's here. I think he can go to the potty by
himself, but I'll let him lean on my shoulder if he really thinks
that'll help."

He said: "You used to be sure of yourself, but very kind."

She shrugged and set out the coffee she had poured for him
without his asking.

"It was your quality. Very direct and funny, but caring."

"Drink your coffee. It's not time to tell me about me again.
That sort of criticism usually ends with: But I'm prepared to
forgive your many sins, in fact more sins than anybody, if only
you'll be nice to me."

He laughed and sat down and put his hands around the cup. It
wasn't hot. Maybe it was breakfast coffee, and that was okay, since
she remembered that he liked coffee in little jolts through the day.
As always, she was right about him, even if he didn't always think
so. She had her way of being surprisingly right.

On the other hand, she had her traditional ways of being wrong, too. Still thinking about poor big-bellied Fred upstairs, he said, "Remember about your father and mother. They hurt you and never knew why, you used to say. They didn't listen to you. They said it was your problem."

"I'm not like that," she said cheerfully, "if you need to remind me. I know when I'm meaning to do harm. I know when I don't care and when I do. In this case, I'm sorry for him, but I really don't care. It's his problem now."

"You weren't supposed to be like that."

Shrug.

"You weren't."

Mouth twitches. This twitch and lifting of the lips always seemed somewhat dramatic to him—her conscious communication of disdain. "You want to fight with me on Fred's behalf?" she asked. "A flush of male solidarity all of a sudden?"

"I'm sorry. I've no rights in the matter, I know.

"It doesn't make sense to start caring about him just now. But—"

"But what?"

"Did I make you like this? Did I start all the troubles that make you like this?"

"And you're not even quarrelling," she asked, "are you? For you this is just a little light conversation over coffee, isn't it?"

"Okay, I talk too much. You're still alive and a puzzle for me, darling."

She smiled and offered him a croissant on a plate. "It's yesterday's," she said, "but I can warm it up. I'll just slip it into this electrical housewife toy that does everything."

The red Warm light went on. She sat at the table—it was their table, one of the things she neglected to get rid of—and smiled at him. There was no reason for his heart to pound. This was not the ruddy, clever, athletic dark creature he had met nearly fifteen years ago. It was not that tall striding woman who had ridden out of college to conquer the world and him. It was a lady with cropped hair, tufts of gray, and a certain experience of the world. She still looked optimistic and hopeful—cheerful because hopes remain to be fulfilled. For good reason she was getting shut of her new husband as she had gotten shut of him, for good reason, a few years earlier. She was smiling and she was hurt and she was disappointed. It returned the soft brave princess look to her face. The woods must be crawling with princes, looking to be kissed. He wanted to say that princes tend to be changed to toads by the kiss; no, changed to husbands—shouldn't she know that by now? She was speaking in her friendly and confidential way to him, only lowering her voice so the man with the sore back upstairs wouldn't be embarrassed. "He comes home tired. He wants to spend twenty minutes talking to me about his day at work. That means holding my hand. I wouldn't mind, but it always stretches to the whole evening and I can't get my own stuff done. I have a sweaty hand. I tell him I like to read, do my own things at night, and I'm willing to make love sometimes—"

He winced.

"—but if I give him twenty minutes, he wants the whole evening. So best is not to give him the twenty minutes. So things do tend to fall apart."

He remembered how, when they were married and their daughter was a baby, he used to follow her around the house, good doggy, when she was tender and sweet, and then he didn't quite notice that she was less tender and sweet, until one evening she said, "Christ! You only spend the day downtown, you'd think you'd been away for a war or something!"

He had become a bore. She needed her own time when the baby was sleeping.

Poor new husband, poor Fred. He remembered her wiggling to the record of "Desire"—late Dylan, glitzy overdubbed rock—as she told him, one afternoon when he came to pick up their child, "Well, I think I've found someone and it's Fred. Probably I shouldn't make predictions anymore, but I think this is it. We talk a lot and we understand each other and"—lots of wiggling to the music that he took personally—"this is it. He's gentle. He's easygoing. He's been hurt, but he's not *damaged*. You should know among the first, of course." He had uttered his congratulations. It was an odd sensation. He felt envy for the happy wiggling and jealousy about the lucky undamaged man and shame for his own failure—not been able to hold her, had he? damaged, was he?—and at the same time something of relief that all doubt was settled. That was odd, but he felt better after Fred moved in; and after the wedding day, when he kept the child for their honeymoon, even better and more settled and resolved. *Easygoing.*

Now he felt pity for the man with thickened middle and sore back and angry jarring down one leg. He too, living the easy life alone in his neat little place, with plenty of time for exercise and regret, had aged these past years. Gray hair and pouched eyes and gold crowns where they showed. So can't Fred do what he did, coast among the young women who enjoy maturity in a man?

Damage isn't so bad. With bed rest, or a little traction and sleeping on the floor, the tingling tends to go into remission.

He reached across the breakfast table and said to her: "I know it's hard. I shouldn't give you advice. Under the circumstances that's just making remarks. Does it sound like a father to you?"

"No," she said, pulling the croissant out, licking her fingers, hilarious, *hot, hot,* it was a little charred—"No, no, dear, like a fucking rabbi!"

Their daughter was downstairs, all sweetly dressed in sweater and plaid skirt and knee socks, very preppy for these times, but she knew it was a look both her mother and father liked, and tentatively, trying out everything in days of trouble, she evidently had decided to leave her cigarettes in a drawer and to please her parents. "Ooh, goody, croissants," she said. "Are we having second breakfast?"

He thought about Fred alone upstairs and said, "Let's finish this one and get going, darling."

"Who you calling darling, Dad? That's a new one on us."

He left a horn of croissant on the plate along with a stiff puddle of honey. He hoisted their daughter's ski bag. He kept a smile on his face. He said goodbye. Their daughter said, "Goodbye and good luck, Mom. Doesn't he have hospitalization and you could move him?"

Outside, he had opened the trunk and slammed it shut before he noticed that his former wife was standing beside him. Their daughter was waiting inside the Volvo. His former wife was speaking rapidly in a low voice, for him alone: "I know you don't think well of me. Why don't you understand?"

"I try."

"Then why don't you?"

"I remember you were the best I ever knew."

"Why can't you ever learn?" she cried. "There's damage!"

STAGES

T HEY MET; he let the crowd move him near her. She said no, no dice, absolutely not, to whatever joke he was making (it was a party); "I don't play those games"; but she licked her lips when he gazed at her. Laser eyes across buzzing space. He heard the no and was sad—he saw her no like the NO! in a balloon from a cartoon mouth—but his shrewd, aggressive, calculating eye also saw her tongue flicking across the shining membrane.

Although an engineer and calculating, he was given to spending his time on love.

Although he looked for a yes like the YES! in a balloon, he was a bit of a scientist.

He tried her again with conversation. Down a step, modest and easy; "Washington is getting out of hand. All the charm of the North and the efficiency of the South—"

"John F. Kennedy said that first."

"I didn't even say it second."

Her tongue flicked. Yes, she didn't know what she did with tongue and lip. Yes, she intended to send her message.

*

At the movies their knees touched. The warmth sheltered them together. She shifted back in her seat. He sighed. He gripped her knee in his hand and waited and then pushed her knee back against his. A swarm of flesh and gesture. He felt strangely shy. He felt like a boy at the movies. Neither of them could remember the movie they saw, something about skiing, or maybe eskimos, there was snow in there someplace, although the warmth of their touching may have been even more fleeting than the shadows on the screen.

*

He knew enough to go slow with this one, a shy and pride-haunted item. He went so slowly that she began to wonder about him. Was he masculine? Was he really a man? But then she would remember his first pressing kisses that she had denied, and his jokes about her mouth closed firmly with a thin white line of no, and his determination to be, okay, if that's how it is, friends. So she had discouraged him? She was worried.

Her elbow looked awkward as she brushed a strand of hair back where it belonged—blond lovely awkwardness—and it fell out of place again. No good doing that.

He was pleased to worry her. She was a modern woman. He gave her "space." To worry in: is that what space is for? Let her take care of her own pride and shyness.

*

Making love, like packing the nostrils of a corpse, to make sure
it doesn't run with awful slime...

He had a therapeutic woman whom he saw more frequently
now that he was in love with a woman who was not an item. He
lost weight. He slept little and dreamed too much. He howled
upon his therapeutic woman. An impatient man, he knew his only
chance was to find ways to pretend patience.

*

She decided to worry (touch of matured feminism) that she
had never invited him to dinner. Sometimes she bought tickets
for something. But perhaps he needed to be really encouraged
after all. She had thought he needed to be discouraged. But like
many men, most men, all men—her plan rolled downhill,
gathering speed—he needed confidence. And only she could give
it to him.

"I'd like to make a light supper Sunday night," she said.

"Before a movie?"

"No," she said firmly,"a literary evening. We'll read the paper. I
have to get up early. I have some sewing. Catch-up time. I'll make
a light supper, oh, I said that already, and you can read and I'll sew
and we'll talk."

"Well, it's true I get tired of restaurants."

She smiled that thin smile of no sex, as he knew it. "You're so
gracious," she said.

And let him think about it from Tuesday till Sunday. She
planned on Sunday to sleep late in the morning, and do a really
good job on her shampoo, and spend more time on herself than
on the food. A little supper, she had promised. A light supper it

would be. A light white wine with sliced pears for dessert. Nothing to interfere with the heaviness of her plan.

She hoped, now that she had made up her mind, he would not dwindle on her. This was the dwindling part of the twentieth century. She knew, alas, all about the dwindlers.

*

He dwindled on her.

They had been at peace and at rest after the light supper. He was reading the New York Times Book Review, the New York Times Magazine, the New York Times News of the Week in Review, the...and her needle was going in and out, in and out, and she moved to get nearer to the light, his light, their light, and her head rested on his shoulder. She was still sewing. He watched her needle darting in and out of the Buttonholes of the Week in Review. He read about the dead testing grounds in Nevada. Dead though they were, they could still send raging growth into the spleen, the pancreas, the chest cavity, the pelvis. Her head felt warm in his shoulder, though it was just clean hair and skull and brain. Smell of blond shampoo and a body he liked.

She put the needle down, sighed, sucked her finger where she had pricked it, turned her head up, kissed him (let him kiss her, seemed to insist he kiss her).

He had put all this behind them. They had switched tracks at Friendship Central. Everything felt cozy. But now he remembered he had judged her sleek freckled healthy arms and shoulders to be exactly how arms and shoulders should be. And now these arms were around his neck, reaching and twisting on the couch. The heavy newspaper slid off the coffee table in cascades of processed data and advertisements from B. Altman. Toes flipped the real estate section—billions of dollars of income property. She was smiling. She was unbuttoning. She was letting him watch her up to a certain point. She was pouting. She was unbuttoning him.

Ah, but he was so scared. His heart was thumping dangerously, humorously. She would have to be helpful. She understood. It was only funny if you thought about it. Now was not a time for judgment and humor. It was not for nothing that she was born into the last third of the century, with all the wisdom of the times absorbed in her bones, marrow, sinew, and tennis-playing blond flesh through movies, song, therapy, and a careful education. Adroitly she had sidestepped a bout with feminism, nodding in passing to indicate it was irrelevant in her case. She smiled. She liked him pretty much, she had decided. She would be helpful. Actually, badminton was her game. She helped and helped, with great confidence and skill.

And goddamn fuck him if he didn't dwindle on her.

"It's all right," she said.

"It is not," he said.

"It's really all right."

"It's really really really not."

She was too smart to try to win this argument. But she had a marvelous idea. Perhaps it was original with her. She jumped up, as if nothing really did matter, and went to the bathroom and left the door carelessly open as she sat on the toilet. She knew he could see. She peed. He looked on dejectedly. Then she turned her back to wash a bit. Somehow, as he looked on, he looked less dejected. He was grinning. Ted the Spy. Some people tend to make too much of things. A toilet is definitely not a pedestal. She came back and sighed and tucked her head into his shoulder on the mussed pillows and deep rug where they snuggled.

Oh-oh.

But she didn't laugh aloud. Peeing at the proper moment, with the door ajar, will never be listed among her inspirations. But it belonged on her real life list.

This time he didn't dwindle on her.

"Oh it was really good," she said.

He didn't reply.

"Really really really good."

She was proud of herself.

                                *

The next day—actually, they skipped a day—she felt slightly displeased when he appeared at her door with flowers, such a macho gesture, and the expectation that she would make a "light supper"—her stiff, teasing oldfashioned phrase haunted her—as before. But he was in a terrible hurry. She was making sandwiches, she opened a can of date-nut bread, she found some cream cheese, and he was all over her. He devoured her. Her body felt slimy, with a fresh rain sleek smell. God knew what it smelled like to him. He seemed to like it. He was drinking and licking her body. Where were they? Were they back where they started? This eager, confident, dangerous kid? Wasn't this what she wanted to avoid, just a playground of sucking and licking and sticking and sexing?

Ah, but she decided to ride with it now. If his voice was too loud when he groaned over her, well, perhaps she wasn't perfect, either.

Maybe this is love, she thought. You don't have to give up judgment. You just have to be engrossed.

She found suddenly she could think of nothing but him, of his body on hers, over and under hers, in hers, and something must come soon to interrupt such an unwanted way of life or she would have to reorganize everything.

"Are we going together now?" she asked.

"I think so," he said.

"Then we can stop to eat the sandwiches."

"Oh I'm hungry."

"I noticed before you did," she said.

Her tinkling laughter sounded artificial to him. It did the same to her. She was ill at ease for weeks. His abrupt recovery, her abrupt cure of him had gone according to plan, and yet nothing that was happening to her seemed like the plan. She was addicted. She grieved in his absence. She was too shy with him, as shy as if she had lost him when, in fact, she had only won him. She wanted to please him utterly.

She was forgetting about herself. For this, the insincerity of her laugh. She was most pleased when he pleased himself. Her body yearned for his pleasure. "Avis tries harder," she said. It was only his pleasure which mattered to her.

And then, because the weather changed, the month changed, or her period came—oh, she didn't know why—her pleasure changed. It was present in her own body. "Oh God," she whispered. "Oh God God God." A squeezing convulsion so like his constricted him from deep within her. And the water broke over

her body, the sweat broke on her thighs like the breaking of the
waters of childbrith.

She lay there gasping. She could say nothing. All that she
wanted to say she preheard in her head and they were words worn
thin by ridicule. *It's never been like this before. I died. I adore you.*

So she said nothing but he knew. And miracle: he loved her
anyway.

*

"That was a doozer," she said.

She tried to talk about it because she thought he wanted to hear
her, but in fact he said less and less about it. This may have been a
sign. She didn't notice. She wished to tell how she felt. As feeling
grew deeper, her words grew more oldfashioned. This one must
have gone back to her parents.

"You're wonderful," she said.

"Doozy is the word, I think," he said. "And wonnerful is what
Lawrence Welk says. A-one, a-two."

"Ted. Don't you love me?"

"I just get sad sometimes."

"Why?"

"I think it's physical. I confuse tired with sad. Maybe I'm only
tired."

"Ted, that was a doozy, but I'd like to do it again, I really would,
so let me help like this—"

She helped.

He smiled. He wasn't so tired after all. She was learning. Even
an adversary stance—he was often an engineer for the offense in
public interest land use cases—could get some good results. It

wasn't that he was paying her back for those months (weeks, actually) of giving him a hard time. It was just that he knew and she knew and both of them knew it was really important in love, if in nothing else in this life, to express and tell and communicate how you really feel, This was California, wasn't it? San Francisco? Her bed?

"Sweet spot," he said once, groaning in her arms.

"That's a tennis term," she said, "meaning the part of the racket where the twang is solid."

He looked at her, terrified and appalled, but then she was laughing and tickling him.

"Won't you allow me to make fun of you?" she asked.

*

She was rather pensive one night. That is, hair lank (blond hair looks almost thin at such a time), eyes chevroned with fatigue, voice small. "What's the matter?" he asked.

"I don't know."

"Never at a loss for words, are you?" he said.

The light came on in her eyes. Anger. "Okay. I have the impression you're keeping a watch on me. I have the impression you're keeping score."

"Well, you're tired, I guess."

"And you?"

"I'm a little tired."

"Then stop keeping score. It isn't necessary. I'll remember you. I do my best to know you. I'm doing my best to let you know me. So don't."

*

The quarrel was mended in a traditional fashion. They decided to go further than they had gone before, and there was no place further in their bodies to go. They decided to take a risk they had never taken, and they took the one left to advanced thinkers who have thought all the advanced thoughts—a daring advance backwards into the tradition.

With double rings they visited a Justice of the Peace in Nevada, laughing all the way. How silly. These days.

Dust all over the hood of the car and crushed insects on the glass and a fan belt that needed changing in Elko, although perhaps the gas station attendant was lying. Elko is famous for supplying unnecessary fan belts. They spent the money gladly. They were gladly rooked. They were happily married.

*

Sometimes the long rain of years seemed to drip drip drip on their happy marriage, a parade without music, a celebration with housework.

But then sometimes she winked at him as she undressed for bed and said, "Now's your chance," and jumped into the clean sheets before he could see more than the flapping of her buttocks. Her legs were slim. Her eyes were clear. Her hair was golden. But she showed him those buttocks and hips, as if to say, Let's be practical. Cool it.

Nevertheless, she still said it was his chance and hers. And he thought that later, maybe months or a year later, she would remember what it was for them. Love. Love. Love.

"That was nice," she said. "Enough. Now I have to get up early and so do you. Now sleep."

She turned over. She wiggled her behind into his lap. He lay curled to her configuration. He lay against the track of her spine. Why couldn't he sleep?

He talked to her; he gave words; he sought to be a husband; he rubbed her back and massaged her scalp; it was not too much of an effort for him. They did the business of marriage together. They made love in the dark. He remembered when they made love with lights blazing.

She lolled in the dreamy prosperity of marriage, pregnancy, child, another child, children. She was as busy as a farm woman with chores. She lay back smiling, efficient, wifely. It was like this, and then almost imperceptibly it changed. She grew pale and tired. They used to have fun.

His gloom? He loved it. It kept his mystery intact. Hers? He clung to her at night, in the dark, when she let him, howling with desire to penetrate mysteries, join flesh, be released of mysteries. She still liked him to rub her back, massage her scalp.

Joy of children. But did she need him now? She had something to think about, and she thought it over and over, until the question began to propose its own answer. *Do I need him now? Why do I need him now? What good is he now?* She meditated this one big question during the long afternoons between carpools and shopping, before he came home—"Hi honey, hi honeys, I'll just shower and be with you"—and then tried to put it out of her mind. And then took to thinking about it in the evenings, also.

She imagined a white knight (horse, golden hair), a black knight (intense unstable eyes), a rock-and-roll ravisher. He imagined her. As she hid from him, and closed off the lease on her body—first the breasts (sore after nursing), then the hips, the buttocks. "I guess this happens to women after childbirth," she murmured. "But you can do it to me."

He loved her. Patience. Wait. Love will come back; is there any reason why it shouldn't? In the meantime, he would survive in his own privacy and in the routines—outings, dinners, chores, birthdays, holidays, inlaws—of a normal marriage. Children.

We'll come out okay, he swore. There was grit and will in this.

All this is wrong about love and what I want, she thought about his silent vows, his grit, his will.

He thought of making love to his familiar wife with Rastaffarian dreadlocks on his head. But what would she wear or do? He thought of her making love to him with black stockings, mouth full of wine, Medusa hair. But who would he be?

Ah we're husband and wife, that's all. People can have fantasies, but we're parents, we're responsible people, we can't play silly games.

And yet he wanted to enjoy the wild in him. *Enjoy* and *wild* are separate worlds. Enjoy is ease and pleasure, wild is risk and excess. He swore life owed him both. But he could not will an amplitude of love from her, though he could conceive of it.

"Do you love me?" he asked.

She gave it some thought. "Sometimes."

"I mean, do you really love me?"

"Are you asking me?"

He looked behind him. Nobody there. Yes, then it was he who was the one that asked if she loved him.

"Okay, it's hard to say. I'll be honest. You're a good man. You're fun. You're a good father. You're...I wouldn't say you're handsome, but that's not a man's thing anyway, and you're fit. Will that do?"

"You sure do get off on the truth, darling."

"Well, what about me?"

Hoarsely he answered: "For some reason you are magic for me."

She shrugged. If he couldn't explain it, how could he expect her to know what it was? All she knew was that magic was someplace, someone, somewhere else. It could be noplace and nowhere. She wasn't going to pretend.

*

FUN

The title of this episode is "Fun." Marriage can be fun, the conservative marriage counselor said. He was perhaps the last marriage counselor in California who counseled marriage. The rest counseled personal fulfillment, making your own space, taking responsibility for your own actions, and dumping that asshole who gets in your way. The counselor's wife was sweet, Irish, Catholic, and had given them three children despite the infantile paralysis which caused her lower limbs to grow increasingly immobile. Her braces clanked, but Dr. Feinberg had fun with his Irish wife. "Marriage is beer against champagne," he counseled. "Beer can be excellent. Champagne tickles, but one doesn't want to live on it. I counsel sexual experimentation, massage, open talk, free play of fantasy, and the enrichment of what you have."

The husband enjoyed this counsel.

This counsel made the wife's lips press together into two white lines. "You can fuck me all you want," she stated, "but I don't like to be kissed."

"We're supposed to get a massage book, for example—here, I've got it, I've also got the oils, unguents, a beach towel, the kids are all asleep, here's a bottle of champagne, haha, I don't just follow what the experts tell me—"

"Not on the lips," she said.

"Look. We have a real investment. We—" and he mentioned children, history, and possessions, trying to tighten his courage toward mentioning once again that he loved her. No doubt that would offend her. He mentioned their house.

"I'm trying," she said. "I can only do what I feel."

"I love you," he said.

"I don't feel anything," she said pensively, wonderingly. "It's peculiar. I'm sure, even with beer, you're supposed to feel something."

"Let me do this—"

"Don't try your technical tricks on me that you learned before we were married."

"I didn't, I didn't! I made them up just now! I want to! I read about them in a book!"

She shut her eyes as if she were remembering a telephone number, turning imaginary pages in her efficient cranial filing system. She was trying to do her part by letting him try his technical tricks. Later she would be angry about this, but now it was important to let him try. She sought to be fair. She knew he deserved this. What she was trying to remember when she shut her eyes was, in fact, a telephone number. The number of another family therapist, one who did gestalt, or was it primal scream; anyway, someone who thought a person should take charge of her own life. When the husband came, the wife was murmuring so he couldn't hear it, *Only way to go.* A phrase she had picked up from a talk show while doing the ironing.

"What? What? What?"

"I told you not on the lips. I think I'd like to see someone else."

"What?"

"Another doctor. A woman in Mill Valley I heard about, dummy." And she patted him on the back almost fondly. She realized he was thinking jealous thoughts and it was nothing like that. And she patted him twice, brief sharp taps, like a wrestler saying, Okay, you can break that hold now.

*

The title of the preceding episode was "Fun," but fun doesn't always turn out to be fun, especially when it is just intended ferociously to be: "Fun."

She got them out of the meddling hands of Dr. Feinberg with his talk of beer and champagne while his wife clanked around in another part of the house.

She got them into the hands of Ms. Suzanne Crowell, B.A., M.A., course work toward the Ph.D., who was frank and hearty and told them to call her Sue and offered to help them both. He thought it might help his wife more to talk alone with a woman expert.

I'll be honest had become one of his wife's favorite expressions.
She was a truthful person, and the truth shall make us free.

*

It all comes together in the dream. Lovemaking as hope, as
expectation, as intention, as ambition, as the building to be built.
And it all came together once or twice, not in memory, not in
expectation, not in memory forward or expectation back, but in
the here and now.

A vacation in the country. Children arranged away. A friend's
house. Rocking, rocking, he penetrated and slid, and her hands on
his back, on his thighs, his eyes locked to hers, her grave face to
his, their grave bodies together, and then both of them smiling,
calm, and then together more, and finally a tumbling collapse
through rushing fever into the abyss of pleasure. Lost. No wonder
they both feared it and craved it. That loss of self.

Yet he knew himself, he felt her, the isolation was ended.

Here. Now.

And it happened more than once as the year went by.

He remembered. It validated. He never could speak properly of
it; he tried; "yes, that was a good weekend," she said. He couldn't
blame her for inadequate words. There were no words.

Rocking and rocking.

It meant he could bear anything now, he thought. Boredom
was not boredom, anxiety was not anxiety, time did not pass, so
strong was their marriage.

They were diligent about marriage. Oh dear. But if you are
serious people, both of you, and you mean the best, how else to do
it right if not with diligence?

If only diligence made people feel good.

Once, when the children were napping, they made love on the kitchen floor and he felt chill bare linoleum against his forehead. Hot below, and a chilled help to his head, and still it was diligent. He thought: If we could get the kids to nap more often. . . .

They had some good times at the movies, too. The cool, the dark, the touching. The stories. The away.

Coming out, they sighed in lobbies. "That was a pretty good one. You want a snack?"

"If *you* will. We don't have to diet."

They both kept fit. This was California. After the movies, what the hell, they enjoyed some Tex-Mex junk food. The spell of dreams. The dreamy lovemaking when they got home.

In the morning, nothing changed.

And then there was a Sunday afternoon when they did all juicy, sucking, desperate, pleasuring things, and nothing good. It was an afternoon when she cried and laughed and bit his chest. It was an afternoon such that it judged all their other afternoons. It was an afternoon of melting, like butter tigers running around the pole, and they lay there exhausted, sweating into each other, breathing, then sleeping.

Before she fell asleep, cuddled into his arms, his arm lightly around her shoulder, cozy, sweet and sour, exhausted, content; before she lost consciousness in the sleep which pulled itself over her like a shutter, she promised herself and swore this would never never never happen again.

*

"Listen," she said, "I don't think you've been listening."

"I'm listening."

"I mean all our marriage."

"Okay, I'm listening."

"I know this is hard."

"Whatever. I'm listening."

She was biting her lower lip in a gesture he had always found endearing. It was not the thin line of refusal. It was when she needed help. "Sometimes I'd rather be with you than with the children," she said.

"I know. I feel the same way sometimes. But you don't look like you're complimenting me, my dear."

"I'm not. I can't divorce the children. So I have no choice. I'm fed up with our life. I have a picture of something else. My picture is childish. I agree. Perhaps I'm wrong. You'll agree with that. But I have an idea of what life can be. I'll be honest with you. This isn't it."

"Okay, okay, okay," he said, hurrying, trying to stop her, hoping she wouldn't say it, knowing she would say it, hoping they would fight it out, hoping this opened the doors, hoping everything could change: "Everything can change. We have too much—"

"We have nothing," she said. "Enough of your blab. I want a divorce."

He stood blabless. She smiled broadly, showing her handsome, large, slightly yellowed teeth.

"That's all right," she said. "I suppose this must be difficult for you. I've given it a lot of thought."

Yes, he thought, no point arguing. She has.

"We'll work it out," he said.

"Did you ever listen to me?" she asked. "I've already talked with my lawyer. Linda Gormley. If you mean to be helpful, it should go easy."

"Thank you," he said.

"Of course," she said, and sighed, "it's never easy. But I appreciate your..."

His what? Paralysis?

"I remember how we were," he said. "I remember those times we cared for each other."'

"How many times?"

"What do you mean?"

"I mean, are you still keeping score?"

SAN FRANCISCO PETAL

J UST ANOTHER funny and pretty little runaway in San Francisco emitting her off-white answers to any questions you ask her: "My father's a gynecologist in Orange, that's Zip Code County, down south, and *so* busy with his patients. Also, I have eight what you might call siblings, and probably you do, so——

"Sometimes I *wonder,* I really ask myself how he takes the way I live my life up north here in San Francisco. But then I realize: *He don't know.*" She giggled, shrugged and touched her pencil to her tongue, probably to wet it.

"It must have really bothered him, finding out about how I wasn't his innocent little thing and stuff; I mean, him being Catholic and all. But I guess I wanted him to find out, otherwise no call to have that kid in my own bed at home with me and everything, especially since Daddy used to come into my room sometimes to plant a kiss on my lips before he made early-

36

morning rounds at the hospital. That's what he was doing that Sunday morning, I suppose. Wow."

She twisted her little head at me over her blue Mexican Marine shirt. "What you thinking?"

"From what you say and how you are, I suspect he knows about your life."

She gazed pityingly at me—that special pity of the 22-year-old countercultural star for a mere orbital astroid. She was slight, lithe, bendable, with freckles on her nose. The little girl in her dressed in a Mexican Marines shirt; the rest of her kept the top three buttons unbuttoned. She smelled of organic food when she breathed near me. She ate carrots for health and orgasmic potency. She dipped them in spiced oil and vinegar, low cholesterol, a shining example to all men. "Whatever he knows," she said, and she fell back into her soft accent for a cool final judgment: "He don't know."

Her temporary profession was waitress at the Natural Sun, soya and no-meat dining for philosophic dope dealers and their clientele. She wore washed-out jeans, of course; flower and butterfly patches, of course. Her shirt came from Goodwill. Those top buttons unbuttoned—good will, too. She may have looked 16, but she knew she was 22, too old to be a legal runaway, and had every right to be sexy, especially since her husband was a drag queen now. He hadn't always been, certainly not in Orange, where he had been the Sunday-morning instrument for imparting news to her daddy, but he kept trying to be more "in" in San Francisco than she was, and she was good at it. So this poor boy from San Diego State, who once planned to go to medical school, now danced and sang with the Cockettes and was the proud possessor of a terrific version of *On the Good Ship Lollipop*. Wilbur called himself Willi. It was so nice and Nazi and camp. Once he'd made it with a Hell's Angel. Linda shrugged. Willi was still searching.

"That's his problem," she said. "But I get along real good with his friends. They accept me. They love to fuss with my hair. Natch, I still don't know if the marriage will last."

I looked up from the menu.

"Oh, we're married legally and all. It happened when we decided to leave—a last act of ole family karma, pal. In a blaze of matrimony, and I wasn't even pregnant, nor ever intend to be. Hey, you like my hair this way, in a flip? They say it's early Fifties, but I don't remember back that far. I think I was bald then."

She was standing by my table. She was waiting to take my order for sprouts, avocado and soy paste on Black Muslim bread. As she talked, she licked her pencil at me; it was not an innocent gesture. I was charmed by her obvious desire to make me fall in love with her, whatever she thought that was, and part-way eager to oblige. I could see neither her father nor me denying Linda anything she really wanted, such as lollipops, spare cash or forgiveness.

Now she was a waitress in an organic-foods restaurant, but she was really busy trying to decide what kind of groupie to be—rock, legal, movie or money. She decided not to specialize and just be a celebrity fucker in general. It wasn't that she was a snob. She just felt turned on by power, and money and fame are power, and isn't that what it was all about?

Naturally, she had to have a sense of humor. Otherwise, why waitress in an organic, no, health-foods place, like a mere wholegrain groupie? Her sign was Capricorn. I told her mine was Exxon.

At this point, the teller of this history must stop to admit he is not merely a historian. He is connected. He has a certain responsibility. He was attracted to the girl in the Mexican Marines shirt who told cute stories of perversion, dope and troubles with her blue VW bus, and once he found her crying in the windowless smoking room of the no-smoking organic eatery.

"What's the matter, Linda?"

"Wilbur."

"What about him?"

"That Hell's Angel. Wilbur wants to leave me."

"Well, maybe it's been heading this way, Linda—"

She was sobbing, her little heart was hurt. "Oh, I knew it would come to no good when he started to run around with Nazis. Oh, I knew it." She was bawling and there were red blotches under her eyes where, if she were older, permanent blue ones might form. "I knew those Nazis were no good, I was a history major, Frank—"

If she had been a journalism major, she'd have known that Hell's Angels are no good, either. Wilbur and his Nazi got married under an AMERICA IS GETTING SOFT poster that depicted two Angels soul kissing. The minister who performed the marriage used to be an Episcopal priest, and he gave lectures now on his mission to the Tenderloin. The band that played had never quite made it during the rock era; they were angry about this and played angry Frisco rock. The *San Francisco Chronicle's* porn editor covered the ceremony. He remarked that it might last as long as some of the marriages he used to cover for what was called the society, then women's, now people pages.

They all floated in their various highs in a meadow far up on Mount Tamalpais, the magic mountain, where the ghosts of extinct Indians—measles? syphilis? drink?—watched over the peacefully browsing Harley-Davidsons and BMWs. Insects thrummed. Birds twittered. Couples coupled.

Although her heart was broken, Linda attended the party afterward. That was brave; it was good form. Her friends expected it of her, and Willi suspected she might. OK, so what? So although her heart was broken, she didn't want to miss the party. She had rejected an offer to be matron of honor, since she was an Orange County girl, raised in the tradition of decorum, where a girl doesn't preside over her ex-husband's marriage to another man, but she wished the new conjugation well. However, she remarked to the leader of the band: "My heart is broken, man. Say, you know I worked as girl Friday for John Lennon when Yoko and he were holed up in the Miyako Hotel. Say, some people think she has like big hairy hands, but they aren't; they're just strong. I really liked her, man. I used to take them fresh o.j."

No matter; the red splotches under her eyes remained; broken heart leads to broken capillaries. Her nostrils were red, too, so if she was up, she wasn't really up, just sniffing a little coke so as to make it through the pastoral afternoon in a meadow on the heights of Marin, nearly 30 motorcycles plowing around, noise, distraction, the full 1973 Angels' Nazi production. There were no human sacrifices today, for the message they brought was love.

I was her date for the afternoon, with hopes of keeping her from despair even if her heart was broken (that's only a mental thing, it heals). I had to get used to the fact that she was completely confident of me but needed a little coke to make sure.

To enjoy the music of 30 motorcycles tearing up a meadow, driven by wild greasers stuck all over with swastikas, leather and metal, you might tend to ask a little chemical aid. I made do with only a deep-seated masochism. I suppose there was a time when I imagined joyful tumblings with Linda, because she seemed to be cute, essence of cute—quiddity of essence of cute—but now I traveled with her in a state of bemusement, merely surprised most of the time, and settling merely to find someone to surprise me. Finally I understand why girls resent men who grab at them first off, demanding bed as the reward for passing their valuable hours. The reason is that they suspect a man can be happy with a Linda, too: just because it's fun to be in her company; or, if not fun, lively; and every man seeks easy friendly funning, too, although he may settle for the distraction of a sweaty roll in the sack.

I didn't give up the idea of sex. I was merely willing to postpone it.

I wondered if I had postponed our lovemaking past its natural moment. I was willing to think of her as a friend first, but maybe she required an immediate kink. The kink who waits becomes a paternal figure—too bad for me.

Or maybe, I prayed, a paternal kink.

It wasn't all one-sided. She gave me a kind of wake-up generosity. As we were leaving the meadow, one of the Angels throomed up on his hawg and grunted, "Hey, Linda. Jump on." Ungh, ungh, ungh.

"I'm with Frank here."

Ungh!

"Dump that creep. Jump."

"Frank's my new old man," she said, hugging me.

He stood there with his eyes bulging as if the leather thong around his neck were too tight. Probably that's why his eyes were bulging; that, plus a little deal with thyroid his metabolism had going; plus maybe the fistfuls of pills he swallowed to inspire his endeavors. He was still leaning there with one pointed hoof prodding the ground.

Linda said sweetly, "You'd have to grab and rape me, and I'm sure Frank wouldn't stand around for that. So you'd have to kill him, too. I know I'm nice, but am I worth it?"

The Angel stared morosely. I could see the motes swimming across his eyeballs. The eyes seemed nearer my head than his.

"Well, I never rape a girl unless she wants to be raped," he said.

"Well, see you, then," said Linda, and she turned, still holding my arm.

How is it not probable that one would be charmed by a girl with such marvelous logic?

Ungh!

"Hey, man." The Angel was calling me. I stopped. Always polite. Linda took my elbow like a school guard and moved me across the daisies.

"Hey, man."

Even she couldn't move me now.

As I looked back, the Angel was smiling and touching himself. "Hey, hear the news? The one-star final, man? Someone died tomorrow."

We went back to her place for a drop of tea, herbal tea, rose hips for a possible nasal congestion. Linda sat down with two chipped mugs and asked nobody in particular: "I wonder if he ever kills a dude even if the dude doesn't ask to be killed?"

"You think they did in that dealer from Texas?"

"I didn't know him personally, Frank. Actually, he was from Oklahoma, if that's where Tulsa is."

"The jury cleared them."

"Then they must be innocent, Frank. I believe in the American judicial rip-off system, don't you?"

Her eyes, if you could see them, were filled with faith. Perhaps it helped to know I was devoted to her, too, just as she was devoted to the jury system. The teller of this story was devoted to Linda because she enabled him to tie in directly, without paying tolls, to the lower levels of his brain, where he smelled girls, sent the blood to sudden anatomy lessons, knew that his throat would fill with blood because of the mental stroke of love. She gave me reality because she was so strange. She kept me in touch with triviality. She dispersed a regular dose of crisis. I wanted to be a disgrace to the life of the mind. Perhaps a good therapist would also receive the hint from all this: Often I just wanted to die. It wasn't just in the middle of the night. It lasted whole weekends or perhaps a whole year.

He.

All this happened to *him.*

Next thing he knew, they had spent a night together. They; we. He discovered groans within his melancholia that no one had told him about. He discovered an ache of desire, and her chilly jokes only made him laugh, they did not discourage him, and he felt very powerful. He smelled the bed, the mattress, her arms. He sniffed and followed his nose. He levitated. He sighed. So now he was a man. He had taken charge. There was no doubt she would love him.

He took her home in the morning. There was an ache of exhaustion, but that made no difference. He slept. He had won something. He telephoned her and there was no answer.

He kept calling and her phone kept on ringing.

Nobody. Nothing.

She disappeared.

Nowhere.

In three weeks, when he had almost given up trying to find her, he discovered that she was living with Van Dixon, the guitarist, in Mill Valley. A redwood house that had been featured in *Rolling Stone,* along with its dripping eucalyptus and mass bathing in the redwood tubs.

He didn't feel jealousy. He was still a different man. No jealousy. He only felt a terrible loss, a blackness of loss; not even desire; just failure, dread, loss, grief.

*

When he finally decided she was never going to call him, he tried one more time. Finally, she spoke with him. She didn't seem embarrassed. She was fine. He was fine. "I'm OK, you're OK." They were cheerful together. "I just came to the conclusion," she said, "a few days in the country would improve my color. I was kind of pale. I should get my energies together. You know, it's kind of freaky, paranoid, in the city. There is a *living space* out here. Not just the trees and all. The aura, man, it's different. So the days just run into the weeks, man."

She didn't mention that what she was running away from in the city was him, was love, was his ignorance. She was talking and confiding how she liked the country and she never seemed to remember that *he* had driven her out across the Golden Gate Bridge; this being-in-love thing, that great night together, they were what finally wiped her out and made her discover a distressing paleness.

At that moment, he knew no other way to be than icy.

"I hear you gave him the clap," he said.

In fact, he had heard they came to the city only to get a shot of penicillin, Van and Linda, together in his Mercedes sedan, both bending over for the needle.

"What?"

"I hear you gave him the clap."

Her sweet laughter. "That's not true," she said. "I didn't give him the clap and he didn't give me the clap. It just happened we both had the clap at the same time."

*

When next he heard of her, she was carrying orange juice to John and Yoko again when they returned to the Miyako Hotel— temporary help; and then she was the girlfriend of an actor who used to be a star, three years ago, and now was only the lead in a TV series, shooting mostly in San Francisco—she was his San Francisco girl; and she had given up organic waitressing.

He saw her having dinner in the Natural Sun, where she used to serve. She had lost 20 pounds, her nose was red and she was just smearing the avocado on her plate, making green tracks with her fork. "I can't eat in this place," she said. "He ripped off my customers."

"What're you selling? Speed?"

"Oh, no, a dirty rotten lie, speed kills. Coke."

"You need to eat. You're sick."

"He ripped off my customers. This place is just a front for coke. I told him about my customers and he ripped them off. I can't eat here."

"You don't look like you're eating at all."

"I can't eat anyplace. They all rip me off." When she smiled, her teeth were yellow, her gums were showing, there were spaces as if her teeth were subtly shifting. He remembered those perfect doctor's-daughter teeth. But the smile was the one she used to dazzle him with and make boredom unboring with. "I'm sorry I ripped you off, Frank," she said. "I gave you a bad time. I don't know how I could, since I'm not worth it, but I guess I did."

"You did," he said.

She waited.

"That's all right," he said, "you're worth it."

He meant he was willing to be ripped off.

"Brave boy," she said. "It was still fun, wasn't it?"

Finally he didn't like being played with. These were words from a scenario and he didn't like them. Not liking them stifled pity. He just got out, leaving the rose-hips tea on his table and the girl who couldn't eat still not eating.

The next time he saw her was in response to a telephone call. "Frank, he's killed me."

When he got there, she was lying on a bed that hadn't been made in months. The place looked as if six Angels had been camping in it, but there was only one, the friend from the wedding, standing over her and holding a glass of water. It was the friend who didn't rape a girl unless she asked to be raped. He looked wobbly. Linda looked as if she were fading in and out of shock.

The Angel glared at Frank with that leather shoelace still tight around his neck. He said: "I tole her to call you."

"My father's a doctor, I know what he did to me," she said. "He broke some ribs."

"She was comin' through all over me. She was, I was tryin' to stop her, what she was doin'. Listen, man, it takes a powerful woman to make me so mean—you calling the pigs?"

"Doctor," Frank said.

He stood there till the doctor came. She would probably be OK if a rib hadn't punctured a lung. When the buzzer rang, the Angel's eyes gave a little extra bulge and he went out the window, just in case. OK, better that way. Frank could handle the explanations.

Linda was finished as a pretty little thing. Whatever came next, it wouldn't be pretty. Frank could go back to saying I about himself.

A DARK NORWEGIAN PERSON

WHEN HE HEARD that his former student Rodman had died on the rocks down a cliff where the sign read Forbidden to Swim Forbidden to Climb Strictly Forbidden his first thought was: *Dummy.* He remembered the young man as the kind of sixties pushme-pushyou for whom the revolution and ardent courtship of his teachers were both part of the same program—the aggrandizement of Rodman. His old-fashioned ambition had dressed itself in the new manners, but the last time they had met, in Paris one summer, Rodman had run up to him, saying, "Dan! How you be, man? Listen, you got to meet my wife, my Norwegian wife, man, I dug up the daughter of about the only Norwegian nonshipping millionaire. Which you wouldn't expect: fantastic in the sack, too."

"This is a big city, Rodman," Dan Shaper had said. "You pick one bank, and I'll take the other, and we don't ever have to see each other, okay?"

"Aw, Dan, why so uptight 'cause an old disciple made it?"
Dummy.

But his distaste had gotten through to Rodman at last it
seemed, or perhaps Rodman simply had no further use for him.
Although they both lived in San Francisco there were no more
attempts at buddyhood, and they never spoke again. The joke of it
was that Shaper caught glimpses of Sigred, the dark Norwegian
wife of his student, and wished he had met this beautiful tall slim
wife with fine straight black hair, a fine straight long nose, pale
cheeks with a few girlish freckles, the slow grace of careful tall
girls when she moved; occasionally he saw her laughing at
Rodman's jokes in a restaurant, in the lobby of a theater and once
on the back of a motorcycle—a rapturous flashing smile that he
remembered and carried with him like an antique postcard from
some rare wonderful unvisited place of pleasure. The wife of his
student who was enjoying a man's games. The wife of a man who
proved his revolutionary fervor by climbing on a private cliff;
small, curly, ever-smiling Rodman, sliding, still smiling and
scrambling, until he smashed on those foam-covered rocks where
the sea lions honked at low tide, where even the ghetto kids knew
it was no place to play macho-man games. The widow of that
dummy.

Shaper did not wait past hearing the news. He wrote her a
note expressing his regret and that perhaps Rodman had mentioned him and that he would call. He telephoned the next day,
and her laughter was light and high for such a tall girl: "You do
not bide your time, do you, Mister Professor?" But before his heart
could quail she added, "I must have some rest of this business. I

might very much like dinner with a person who is not involved. Tonight would be best for both of us, would it not?" The laughter again: "You because you are so impatient. Me because I do need distraction, dear solicitous kind friend."

When he came for her it was not a house of death. The color of mourning was only in her hair; her dress was white, a dazzling crocheted material that clung to the long limbs; she wore no jewelry—perhaps out of respect for her husband—but the effect was to emphasize the brightness of teeth, the caves and shadows of breasts, bones, sea-colored eyes; even the faint pale down of her arms glimpsed through the long loose sleeves. Of course she still wore her wedding band.

"Sit." He perched. "May I offer you some wine? I don't know what I'll do with all the wine our friends have brought me."

"No thank you," he said.

"Perhaps you would like a bottle or two to take out for your own cellar? German wine, Rhine wine, May wine, I seem to have a great many sweet wines in stock these days."

"Maybe you'd just like to get out," he said. "I mean—"

"It's all right. Look around you." And as he followed this order he saw very little sign of Rodman. There were spaces on the walls, there was the sense of a roommate having recently moved. "I asked his friends to take souvenirs of him. I called the Goodwill for the rest. Naturally I have kept a few books, some pictures. But what else should I do?"

He did not answer, and she shrugged.

"Before you express your condolences in the manner of some of his friends, let me say that we were about to separate, I wanted a divorce, I didn't know how to make him give up. And I know you didn't like him, he complained about you, you were a toothpick in his arm"—odd expression—"and that's why I accepted your invitation. Please, Mr. Shaper, no bullshit."

He focused on a floating mote. He did not know where good manners would place his stare.

"Not that I am not sad. Of course I am sad for the poor soul, poor selfish lost soul, poor poor sad silly boy."

Her eyes filled with tears. The tear in each eye seemed to swell like a gigantic contact lens, without falling, and abruptly she stood up, and her long sure stride took her to the bathroom. The water ran. When she returned her face had been scrubbed, her cheeks shone, she was smiling. He had been in love before he saw her. It was not love, of course, it was infatuation with beauty, perhaps complicated by spite for an irritating young man with unmerited good luck; Dan Shaper, himself, considered his fate in marriage to be unmerited bad luck. But what he felt for her now was respect for her lack of hypocrisy, admiration for her straight-forward honesty. He desired her. He even felt some grief for the suffering she tried to not allow herself. It welled up in her anyway. He loved this girl.

He remembered a sabbatical visit to Norway, all those fine-haired, fine-eyed people, friendly and polite until they got drunk, and then the bloody fights over a taxicab while wives or girlfriends huddled and watched, and then either the police screeched up in little black patrol cars to haul them away to sleep it off, or they simply picked themselves up off the street, bowing, shaking hands, offering each other a congratulatory drink for a slugfest well slugged. Crazy people in their sensible way. Of course, he had not met a girl of Sigrid's world-traveled, moneyed class. She might be crazy in her own way, he thought as they talked through a fish dinner at Seoma's (petrale, salad with just lemon, a bottle of white wine, fruit and cheese for dessert—a light dinner for the recently bereaved), but she also seemed to him the sanest person he had met in years. As for craziness, Shaper could supply all they needed. It was crazy to feel the way he felt for her, like a boy. It was crazy to admit it to himself and, given her sharp eyes, to her. It was crazy to not care that he was crazy and to take such satisfaction in it.

She enjoyed laughing at him.

"Rodman," she said, "he was so jealous he wanted me to stay in the room while he composed. Have you ever sat for hours, days, while a songwriter picked at a guitar? A Zen Buddhist country-rock composer? A ballad in favor of saving our water power, adopted from the original Japanese rockabilly tune? An untalented ambitious clever boy?"

He touched her hand.

"And have you ever had a lover who wanted to keep the bathroom door open for conversation? To talk to you? At least I hope that's why. He even took the lock off the door. Maybe," she said, wrinkling her brow, "maybe he liked. . . to watch. . . . No, I think it was just Rodman's jealousy. Perhaps was I hiding something in there?"

When he touched her hand she squeezed his fingers with her own long warm slim ones and did not hurry to let go.

"I'm so sorry for him," she said. "He found the wrong wife, the wrong way of life, the wrong death. He admired grand suicides, you know. Very romantic person. I think his death was not even provisionally grand. And even," she said, he waited, "I even believe it was mostly an accident. I am going on that assumption."

"You're a firm person," he said.

"I try my best. I do what is required. I deeply regret some things in the past. I do my best to go on."

There was no question about where they would go or what they would do after dinner. First they had a little walk by the bay, along the embarcadero. For Shaper it was a good augury, no particular reason why, that they saw a Norwegian freighter shining, a bit scummy, in the late summer remnants of daylight-saving daylight. The disappeared sun, still reflected in the low rim of fog through the Golden Gate, made faint diamond glints against the portholes. She took his arm.

They drove to his flat in an old house on the steep, quarried slope of Telegraph Hill. Women sometimes commented on how lucky he was to have found such a place, and then he had to say it was hard to carry groceries up, but, yes, he was lucky, and then they would talk about fireplaces, about books, about views, about the pleasant detritus of a fairly long life. She skipped all this. They stood and looked back at the darkling city, and then they looked at each other, and then he led her into the other room.

No, it seemed as though she was leading him. "I hear your heart!" she said. "Please, don't be nervous. Please to please yourself, Sir, and you can be quite sure I will be happy. Please!"

Because he seemed so nervous she slipped off the tiny filmy bra first. He helped her with the dress, she said, Ouch!, and she laughed, and he laughed, and they both laughed when she said, Wait! as the crocheted material caught on one erect nipple.

His nervousness passed.

The night passed.

In the morning, when he awoke, she whispered to him—she must have been awake awhile already—"Poor Rodman. This is what he feared, he so much dreaded." She touched his lips with her fingers, fingers that smelled slightly of their lovemaking, and he kissed each finger in turn. "But not with you," she said. "You were one he never feared, he only wanted you to like him a little. Perhaps now you do."

*

Since his divorce, since his loss of the wife he had mourned so long, Shaper had treated love-making as a way to say good-bye. It eased him. It said, *Okay, so go,* to that lost wife. Lovemaking should not be a way to say good-bye, but that was how it was for him.

His first lovemaking with Sigrid was a hello to something new. It was only a beginning. He thought of her. He thought of no other woman. Ah, perhaps he thought a little of himself and of Rodman, but only because poor Rodman had led him to Sigrid, and Sigrid had led him back to himself. And the spiral was complicated but complete. He could forget himself and think of her.

So far he could not tell if she thought of him. When love is fresh, or so it seemed to Shaper, that does not matter so much. Eventually it matters very much. It matters the whole world. Eventually it was a matter of life of not life, life or what Shaper had been living until he met Sigrid, that she begin to love him.

Pillow philosophers sometimes write that the important thing is to love, not to be loved. They emit a steady hum of benevolent nonsense, advice for self-help manuals, framed, fake parchment sheets, the poesy of broccoli-headed teenagers. I'm running on, he thought. What's the subject?

Shaper's avid hunger had been reawakened overnight. After the famine and fast and the years of stolid acquiescence in a poor regimen, he wanted once again what everyone wants. It was good; he was sure of that. It even allowed him to feel kindness for poor Rodman, a little pity for his loss, something like human respect for the boy. And one hell of a lot of gratitude. Inadvertent favors may be the best ones.

They spent the day together. They went to a museum in the morning, like kids courting: French impressionism plus not enough serious looking to tire their feet. He felt light and floating; the morning's cold shower lasted all morning. Then they sat at the counter of a shellfish bar and ate clams, shrimp salad, drank little bottles of cold beer, and she said it was like a Norwegian lunch except there were no little squares of buttered bread. No matter. They ate little crackers and broke off chunks of sourdough French bread. Then she had to see her lawyer, something about the will, something about taxes and probate, and he drove her to Montgomery Street.

Now the shower was used up. He was sweating with desire for her—her athletic back and long legs rapidly retreating into the foyer of an office building—and it was good to have an hour to catch his breath. Finally he remembered to call the department secretary at the university and tell her he would not be meeting office hours today. Suddenly, in her absence, he was gasping for air, as if they had run a race, as if he had drunk a whole thermos of black coffee; it was no rest at all to be without her.

He remembered that she had wanted to divorce Rodman because he could not live without her.

When she returned, smiling and easy and carrying a legal-size envelope, he smiled back just as easily and welcomingly. He felt cured.

"You always smell so sweet," he said. "You know what someone said about the California blond? She can ride forty miles in the back of a pickup truck and still smell delicious."

"You forget I was born in blond country," she said.

"You smell that way."

"But we dark ones have to work at it, I think," she said, laughing into his eyes and poking at him. She took a fistful of his hair and pulled. "You're dark, and you don't bother."

"Where's your truck?"

"Tak tak tak," she said. "It's not fair, but thank you. Now let's have a nap. I need—after the lawyer, such questions!—I need a dream or two."

"All I can promise is one," he said because he wanted to hear her laughter, and he knew he could promise her and himself all they required, all that was necessary to forget lawyer and probate and Goodwill, all that was past and painful and insignificant; he felt strong enough with her to provide all the sweet dreams in town. Life was intended to be this garden for those who made it so.

*

A week passed. They spoke of Rodman. She didn't want to meet Shaper's friends. "Remember I'm in mourning," she said.

That was all right with him. He wanted her all to himself anyway. He didn't mind if she spoke of Rodman at odd moments. It was natural, it was touching, it was sad, it had brought them together. Once he peeked in a closet and saw that, indeed, she had given his clothes to Goodwill. A few hangers clanged together like a broken piano when he brushed them. When one fell he saw a single, forgotten sweat sock in a dark corner. Poor Rodman. Lucky Dan.

He spoke a little of his former wife. She listened patiently. He admitted he had loved his former wife. She listened patiently. He told how he had suffered when she needed her freedom, she needed to change her style, she needed up, out and away. Sigrid listened patiently.

He caught on, being reasonably intelligent, to the fact that none of this interested Sigrid in the slightest. It had not brought them together. It was stale news. It had nothing to do with their lives now, or so she thought, however important he might consider it. He was not too stupid. He shut up.

One more time, and it was only in the dark, near four in the morning, he found bereaved widow's eyes staring at him across a bleak snowfall of sheet and pillow. When he started to awake to comfort her she shut her eyes and seemed truly to be asleep. He was not sure if it was his dream or hers that had awakened him or her.

That morning he watched her pick up the snails in her garden and throw them into the street. "They'll sneak back at night," he said.

She shrugged. "Then I shall have to throw them out again. Do you like my garden? I don't grow vegetables, only mint and flowers."

He liked her garden.

At the end of the week he had to make a three-day trip to Denver for a meeting of experts in his field. It was not the usual airport conference to exchange reports, papers and expense accounts. "It is," he said ironically, "an in-depth, three-day meeting. I'll miss you."

"Yes," she said.

"Will you miss me?"

"Why else would I be here?" she asked. They were in his bed; no, they were in her bed, the bed she had shared with Rodman; of course she cared for him.

Don't press, don't press, he thought.

"That's nice," he said.

A little later, stroking her back, kneading the long skier's muscles, he asked, "Will you miss me?"

"That was nice before," she said. "Turn over, and I'll do for you, too. Come on, turn over, your turn."

He submitted to those long strong kneading fingers. Oh, good, good, good. How cleverly she had guided him into not insisting on the wrong question, the wrong prying, and yet gave him what they both wanted. How intelligent. How good.

"It's all right I'm leaving for a few days," he said. "It's important. It's too much otherwise."

"Shush," she said. "Just feel what I'm doing with my hands. Let your back be alive, and that's enough."

"I never thought I'd feel so good again."

"Shush."

"I don't remember anything like this. I don't remember anything before you. Why am I going to Denver?"

"The Brown Palace is a beautiful hotel. I love the light in the central hall—you call it central hall? You will do good report and answer other people's questions. Now turn a little this way and shush."

He lay in silence awhile.

"See," she said, "you are you, and I am I. That is very good, dear."

"Everything is good now. Use my name. Don't call me dear. Speak it."

"Now I relax your legs like so. Shush."

"Speak it. Use my name."

Silence.

"Speak it."

From down below where she was smiling and pulling at his legs, pressing her thumbs against the inner slab of thighs, bending, letting him feel her long hair brush against him, her warm breath, she said stubbornly:
"Dear."

*

Nevertheless he separated himself from her, scraped clean inside with joy and also exhausted and nerved by desire, his body trimmed down and tensed by the effort of pleasure. He had expected nothing more like this in his life. Stan, an old friend, a colleague of other expense-account festivals, a veteran of two marriages, looked at him at the conference registration desk in Denver and said, "You've changed! Oh oh, one more gray hair, but you look so much younger—you look like a kid!"

"I've found someone," he said.

"That'll do it ever time," said his pal. "God's stacked dex. I think I've paid for that mistake by looking younger a few times, too."

"No, really."

"I agree it's wonderful. I do. See me turning moldy colors? Hey, pal: Getting married? Living together? What's happening?"

"I just met her. Her husband just died." Unwillingly he added, "He was a student of mine a few years ago."

Stan sent him a pitying, sarcastic, jealous stare. Out of his own hunger, in a lobby full of people peeling off the backs of their identification labels, he gave him this naked look. Stan said, "What's good is good. We'll see. You are pure enchantment, my man." And he slapped his label to his jacket above his heart.

Shaper took the elevator to his room in the Brown Palace Hotel of Denver and wrote a letter although he would be home to her by the time she received it. But he wanted to tell her about meeting Stan, poor, funny Stan, who hadn't gotten over an infatuation with blacks' natural sense of rhythm, a graduate-student disease; no, he wanted only to tell her about her long lean gawky legs, her graceful skinny arms, that lank fine black hair, the lemony taste of her kisses, the damp cool warm idiotic peace of his dozing against her back, her belly, the curve of her throat, wherever he tumbled, of what his friend Stan the Spoiler tried to say to him, of his final triumph in not looking back to his wife, of his even greater triumph in not looking forward to any plan at all for the future, only for tomorrow, the day afer tomorrow, the day after that. . . . Perhaps she didn't know all these things. It was unnecessary to sort it out. Perhaps she had

other matters on her mind—of course she did—and didn't need to
be called to order.

Careful, he thought.

He actually wrote the letter and carried it downstairs to post so
that, with luck, she might receive it on the morning of his return.

He was smiling and clever and useful at the meeting in the
Rocky Mountain Room of the Brown Palace Hotel. Stan and he
had no further conversation about anything but Stan and the
conference. This seemed wise.

He did not drink with his colleagues after the meetings.
Leaving, he received a blessing from Stan, a tap on the left
shoulder, *I dub thee Sir Dude Courageux,* and he proceeded to bed
upstairs of the raucousness and slept as easily and calmly as if her
lemony breath had been breathing into his mouth.

He took the early plane home.

There was no answer when he telephoned her. Well, that was
okay. He hadn't told her which flight he would arrive on. But
nevertheless he was disappointed because he had funny things to
tell her, and now they seemed stale. He had bought a book of
rodeo drawings at the Denver airport, and it seemed stale. He had
written a note to her on the back of a postcard showing a rope-
twirling contest at the University of Wyoming and put it between
the pages of the book of rodeo drawings. "Higher Education in the
Far West. B.A. in Broncobusting, M.A. in Corral." Stale.

He called an hour later, just before dinner time, no answer. If
she had an appointment with a lawyer it should have been over by
now. But of course she had lots to do. Surely her friends were
keeping her busy. He knew nothing about her friends, of course.

He imagined one of Rodman's grief-stricken friends putting an entirely natural make on her.

He called later in the evening. He let it ring although that was foolish. When he put the phone down it went on ringing in his head, and his joke about higher education in the Far West seemed terribly stale and foolish and Stan-like. And this was reality. Such was really the case about his attempt to be young and cute for her.

He called at midnight.

He decided to not call again till the next morning, but he called at 2:00 A.M. and let the phone ring and ring.

He went to the bathroom and looked at a haggard face in the mirror. He slapped his cheeks lightly. He tried to think of his former wife and the pleasure they had once taken in each other. It was like remembering a favorite movie, finally seen once too often on a late-night channel. He thought of Sigrid, but there was very little to remember it seemed, very little to think about, and yet he could think of nothing else.

He looked for something of hers in the bathroom. Nothing. No, a shadow of her—a fine honey soap she carried in her purse the first time. For the dark girl who smelled sweet in the back of a pickup. It was dry and barely used, and the indentation MIEL D'OSLO was sharp.

She didn't answer in the morning, either.

That day he finally awakened her at noon. Her sleepy voice. Her lemony breath. Even over the phone he could taste her breath. So there were other things to hold besides the honey soap.

"I've been calling!" he burst out. "I've been calling!"

"Hi. I suppose so," she said sleepily

In a spasm of sanity he said nothing and waited.

"I'm sleepy," she said. "It's so hard to explain things when you're asleep. My husband died a week, no, I guess it was almost a month ago. Time passes so fast anymore."

He waited. He listened. She sighed, trying to wake up.

"I've found someone. Don't worry, he's not here now. Oh, I'm so sleepy, I wish I were awake for this talk you require, I meant to be. Okay. I'm awake now."

He listened to his cool politeness. "Would you rather I called later?"

"No. No. Dear, you're wonderful, but I found someone else. I like him pretty much. We used to ski with him. He's just, well, he's a good cross-country skier. Dear, I'm sorry, I'm not ready for wonderful I guess."

"I'm not," he said.

"Yes, yes, you are, I really think so."

"That's a"—no, he wouldn't say *mean*—"that's a cunning thing to say, Sigrid. It's just you like him more. That's all. He's wonderful."

Now she was silent. Her turn. She was better at it. She was stalled by his petulant and stupid rage. She had no grief in her.

"Don't you remember?" he asked. "Don't you remember!" he burst out.

"How would you know what I remember? What makes you think I even like you? Now I must hang up," she said, and she did.

BART AND HELENE
AT ANNIE AND FRED'S

I T WAS A party to celebrate the coming together and going together of two lovers who surely deserved a good time after their recent bad times. Fred's wife had left him for the organic baker down the street. Annie's husband had not left her, but he really should have made the decision she finally made—he forced her to make it—leaving him for Fred, who hung about the village library after his wife's defection. Fred had moped a lot until Annie consoled him. Now they were happy, and everyone was eating grape leaves wrapped around meat and bread crumbs and drinking white wine, and the party looked like a party for slightly thickened college kids. They were no longer college kids. The thickness was mostly not in the bodies, only in the faces and jaws, since in California one jogs, one plays racquet sports, one skis, one keeps fit. Annie and Fred were a fit, newly happy couple.

Bart was glad for Annie and Fred. He sat on a pile of foam covered with fur, leaning against the wall and fingering the extruded nipple of an empty plastic wineglass. He would have risen for a refill, but he didn't want to lose his place on the improvised couch. He was pleasantly bone weary from a late afternoon at racquetball, and he was interested in talking with the very tall, excessively broad-shouldered outdoor goddess seated next to him. She turned to offer him wine from her glass, and they got through the introductions, professions—he a lawyer, she a psychology instructor at the community college—and the first affable joshings and seriousness. She was a fine-looking woman with heavy sun lines around the eyes and on the forehead, skin etched by sun. He liked her, he wasn't interested in her, he felt at ease with her, he would just drop here for a chat.

Helene told him she had spent five years in the Peace Corps in Brazil. Bart told her he was the oldest man at the party, an observation he freely made these days, and she replied that she was thirty-nine. He said, "You look it, but that's good," and she laughed, and he said that anyone under fifty looked young to him (not true), and he told her he was forty-seven. And thus they fell to talking about being alone at night, or on the party circuit, or having trivial—"Quadrivial, Madame!" he said—connections at their ages.

It didn't even seem odd to be so frank with a stranger—"You're the only stranger I know," he said.

She said she was tired of "boys"—men little older than her students, "sensitive" sometimes, but not knowing very much, or not enough, so that after she finished her days as a teacher, she spent her evenings teaching, too. She ended these relationships after a trip to Hawaii or into the desert or up a mountain or anyplace, she said. They didn't survive more than a few whole days together, even with some active sport to bring them together.

"I know," Bart said. "I don't live with women now. I travel alone—that's your mistake. I confine myself to..."

Helene smiled.

"A few hours at a stretch," he said.

Helene didn't seem very sexy to him, but he found himself making erotic insinuations to her. He didn't mean to tease. It just came out like that. He felt a little tired in a pleasant way. She was a nice stranger.

Everywhere else in this cottage on a hillside, filled with furniture scraps and people, unfurnished because other spouses still had custody of such things, other new couples and new noncouples were eating folded grape leaves, drinking white wine, making jokes, constructing plans for later, all pleased for Annie and Fred whose finding of each other they were celebrating, all interested in what erotic surprises such a happy occasion might bring. A few talked about their businesses and the economy, their professions and the economy. Annie and Fred circulated with plates and jugs Annie's face visibly flushed with pleasure despite the discordant disguise of disco makeup, Fred's face quite pale and worn with all the joys he was suddenly being forced into; they made a nice pair, one so determined and strong, the other so recently unhappy and now gratified, being taken care of. Once Fred tried to refill Bart's plastic glass and Bart said to him, "Buddy," and Fred answered, "You told me, Bart, you told me everything would be all right, you were the one who told me."

"Your attorney wouldn't lie," said Bart, "that would be un-ethical."

He didn't express, however—though he might to Helene in due course—his doubts about a recent wife who took up with her new true lover and yet kept herself hidden behind the makeup strategies of a punker. "Maybe she's insecure," Helen would no doubt reply.

Fred moved off with a pleased wan smile at Bart and Helene, at his friend and Annie's friend, who were so obviously and seriously exploring the worlds of hope and possibility on the temporary heap of foam.

Helene and Bart found themselves making little alternating speeches about their experiences in love. Bart had the comfortable sense that these were not serial monologues, plaints and brags, but rather a sort of leisurely dialogue. He was interested in her story. She seemed interested in his. When one interrupted, the other waited, answered, and completed the story.

She had had a serious lover in the Peace Corps, another her first years in Berkeley. Serious love affairs break up as shatteringly as unserious ones; more so, of course.

"Of course," he said. "I've had that experience."

Patiently and kindly she waited to see if he wanted to take the initiative with his own story. He didn't yet. She went on to describe the increasingly unserious love affairs, unserious at least to her, in which she led young men on pedagogical expeditions and felt lonely after the strong smells of athletic boys had been aired out of her flat.

"That's not unserious," he said.

She waited and he waited, so she gave him an example—the lad with whom she had just broken up. He didn't read worth a damn. She thought he was bright. But he was just "into music," and nothing she could do—

"I find it's a mistake to try to educate the young," he said. "Better to accept them simply, without trying to be one among them, of course."

"Otherwise you become a parent," she said, smiling.

"Or a teacher," he said, smiling.

They smiled at each other. They were holding hands. How had this happened? he wondered. He wasn't really interested, though he liked her a lot just now and it was cozy here with her on the pile of foam, being ignored by the standing and shifting bodies that filled the room.

It would be rude to let her hand go. Her hand was dry and warm and strong and nice, even if he wasn't much interested in more than resting here after his recent exertions at racquetball and talking with a canny and sad woman going through some difficult times in life. He too was going through a difficult decade or generation or, anyway, something difficult, without necessarily being wise. He was just himself, and that was what he had to work with.

She smiled expectantly. She was looking at him with sun-crinkled, sun-washed eyes that asked: And now you?

He disengaged his hand from hers, reached for her glass, and took some of her wine. The gesture felt like a necessary apology for what he was about to say—a gesture of friendly intimacy in advance.

"I like young women," he said. "I like their smell. I like their expectancy. But mostly I like that they haven't been hurt. I think I could like older women, too, because I know some I like, and they smell sweet, too, but the older women of that sort, the great ones, are all claimed. They have men. And the ones that don't—"

"You don't want to live with their bitterness," she said.

"I don't have to, so I don't."

She did not grow angry. She went on smiling as if this were the nicest thing in the world to hear, what she had always wanted to hear. "Naturally you want only the great ones," she said.

"One great one would be enough."

"So lacking her—"

"It's easier for me," he said, "than it is for older women. It's simply a fact that I'm not disqualified. You're not either, you're special, smart and talented, but it's easier for men. We don't have to be special to be in luck, in a kind of luck. Which doesn't mean, of course, that I haven't had some miserable spells of grieving over women—over one woman, as it happens in my case—only I've given up grieving in public. In public I've developed good cheer."

"Imitating good cheer tends to mean you feel it."

"Thank you, Professor. Yes, you're right—"

"William James was right."

"Both of you. Cheerfulness spreads, that's right, to the inner being from the outer action. Hypocrisy turns out to be more valuable than we used to think in the Summer of Love."

They toasted hypocrisy, she with her plastic glass of white wine, he with his clenched fist. She drank first; then he took the offer and drank again from her glass. He got up and refilled her glass and a fresh one for himself. When he returned, he said, "The main thing I notice nowadays is that I don't fall in love anymore, I don't get infatuated, I just enjoy the young women who can put up with me. My kids—children—take a lot of my time. I even enjoy good relations with my former wife. If love is an attempt to complete the inadequate in ourselves, well, I seem to be reconciled to my own inadequacy without love. Or at least to the fact that love won't cure it. And so—if you'll forgive the vanity—I give the impression of security. I don't care. I don't care enough to be insecure, but I like the good tastes and good natures of some young women."

She smiled to indicate that she forgave the vanity, perceived the inadequacy, liked him. Her teeth were large, squarish in front, regular.

"My lovers are all looking for mothers or teachers," she said. "I think some of them mostly like eating my food, using my washing machine for their T-shirts and jeans." He laughed. "I'm not kidding," she said. "They like to save their quarters for records."

"You're a nice person," he said. "You're grown-up. You're intelligent. You're decent. You're pretty."

He meant everything but the last, though she had a kind of appeal in her large boniness. Her hand tightened on his. He wished for her to be his friend, even very briefly, even for the time remaining before he would head home. To say she was pretty was not a reprehensible lie. For some men it would not be a lie at all.

He looked at his watch. He had expected to leave before now. She was keeping him up late. She caught his eye and smiled. They were leaning against each other. Her shoulder radiated warmth. "It's later than we think," he said.

She sighed.

"No one is interrupting us," he said.

"They think we're together."

He sighed, too. He stood up. He said, "It really is late. I played racquetball. I have to be up early to take my kids to, you'll not believe this, Sunday school. Honest."

"I understand," she said, and she understood.

Because they were honest and understanding with each other, he did not ask her telephone number. He saw no need to imply any lies. He would not call her. He had already forgotten her last name. He held her hand as she remained seated and he said, "I really liked our conversation. It was good to talk with you."

He had no idea what she was doing when he walked away. He didn't look back till Annie and Fred came to thank him as he thanked them for having a good time at their party. Helene had already vanished from the foam temporary couch.

CAPRA BACK-TO-BACK SERIES

1. URSULA K. LE GUIN, The Visionary, *and*
   SCOTT R. SANDERS, Wonders Hidden

2. ANAIS NIN, The White Blackbird *and*
   KANOKO OKAMOTO, The Tale of an Old Geisha

3. JAMES D. HOUSTON, One Can Think About Life
   After the Fish Is In The Canoe *and*
   JEANNE WAKATSUKI HOUSTON, Beyond Manzanar

4. HERBERT GOLD, Stories of Misbegotten Love *and*
   DON ASHER, Angel On My Shoulder

5. RAYMOND CARVER and TESS GALLAGHER
   Dostoyevsky (The Screenplay) *and*
   URSULA K. LE GUIN, King Dog (A Screenplay)

6. EDWARD HOAGLAND, City Tales *and*
   GRETEL EHRLICH, Wyoming Stories

DON ASHER

Angel on My Shoulder

Stories

CAPRA PRESS
1985

Cover design by Francine Rudesill
Design by Jim Cook
Typography by Cook/Sundstrom Associates

Gratitude to the National Endowment for the Arts
for their valuable assistance.

LIBRARY OF CONGRESS CATALOGING IN PUBLICATION DATA
Gold, Herbert, 1924-
STORIES OF MISBEGOTTEN LOVE.
No collective t.p. Titles transcribed from individual title pages.
Texts bound together back to back and inverted.
I. Asher, Don, 1926-   . Angel on my shoulder 1985.
II. Title.   III. Title: Angel on my shoulder.
PS3557.034S7   1985   813'.54   85-7756
ISBN 0-88496-234-2 (pbk.)

PUBLISHED BY
CAPRA PRESS
Post Office Box 2068
Santa Barbara, Ca. 93120

CONTENTS

1. Angel On My Shoulder / 7
2. The Barrier / 46

ANGEL ON MY SHOULDER

THE WEEKLY cross-continental calls, Worcester to San Francisco, commenced in the fall of 1975. My mother had just passed ("celebrated" was not a word she would have used in the context) her 87th birthday. She felt she wanted to speak to me once a week from "here on down to the end of the line, " and we set a time of Sunday noon, PST. She'd do the calling. "You don't even have to remind yourself. It's on me, my responsibility. From all I hear about your profession, they don't pay musicians in IBM certificates." This was (1) an allusion to her sizable blue-chip stock holdings (half of which would one day come to me: shares purchased in dribs and drabs since 1930, when my father died, and staunchly held regardless of the bull's charge, the bear's hug), and (2) a not so subtle dig at my having abandoned a career in chemistry to play the piano in dance halls and saloons for the *shikkers* (drunkards) and *nafkas* (disreputable women). Both my father and older brother had been chemists,

7

graduates of Worcester Polytechnic Institute; in the forties scions of the Jewish middle class tended to follow in sharply-defined footsteps.

"Just remember to be home twelve o'clock noon Sundays, so I won't be saying 'I can't hear you, talk louder' into your machine."

"I'll be here. How are you feeling?"

"Mark, dear, I'll tell you something"—Mark is my brother; this was scarcely a harbinger of senility, she's been switching our names, Mark/Jay, for half a century—"I'm 87 years old. I'm not half bad, considering. But the old grey mare ain't what she used to be."

Mark, who lives less than a mile from her and looks in on her daily, told me that she's frail, her eyes have been failing for the past couple of years, and a good part of her days are taken up with small battles of vision. The furniture in all the rooms has been pushed against the walls. She reads her mail (but is gradually giving up on newspapers and magazines) with a powerful magnifying glass. Phoning involves a laborious counting of holes in the dial. When using the electric stove she fingers the notched arrows that indicate low, medium, high, and recites an accompany ing litany: "counterclock, higher heat." Mark has proposed hiring someone to come in a few hours a day to do the housework and cooking (and relieve him of shopping chores). She won't hear of it. "I don't want anyone in this house, I'm not giving up my privacy." And less vehemently: "Blind people cross streets, work at jobs. I'm going to be a good trouper..."

Those eyes. In sepia shots taken before I was born they shone with a warm lambent light that seemed to come from far back.

When I had last seen her in the late sixties they were the eyes of Indira Gandhi or Albert Einstein: hooded, pensive, sorrowful. Two decades earlier when I was in high school and first started playing the piano in taverns and strip joints along the Worcester Turnpike she used to wait up for my one/two-in-the-morning home-comings, face framed in the parlor window, backlit by a lamp's dim yellow gleam. With that anxious doleful gaze, touched with resignation (advance intimations of the good trouper), she looked like a figure in an old Flemish painting—as if she had been there beyond time, solid and sorrowful, keeping vigil. I had begun drinking in my junior year—nothing too serious, ale, beer, an occasional Mr. Boston gin and Coke. I took precautions with my breath, but a carton of Sen-Sen wouldn't have helped: I trailed in the front door with me, like the cloud accompanying the L'il Abner character Joe with the surname of jumbled consonants, a reeking nimbus of saloon fumes. Her lips parted as she met me in the hallway; a lengthy sigh slipped from them, an exhalation as fragile as the satin rustle of a stripper's dropping garment, and her greeting never varied: "Dear God in heaven, you smell like a brewery." An uncle had once told me, "There are two things that never passed your mother's lips: a dirty word and a drop of whiskey." The observation was validated by my father's closest friend, the eminent playwright S.N. Behrman—they had grown up together on Worcester's Providence Street hill—when he wrote to me on the occasion of my bar mitzvah: "My dear Jay, I had no idea that you were getting to be an old man. I didn't think you would be bar mitzvah for years yet but here you're creeping up on me in your quiet way. The traditional bar-mitzvah gift is a

watch. I am not sending you one because for all I know you have a watch. I am sending you, therefore, a check so that you can buy yourself something you like. Don't spend it on liquor because your mother has never liked drunkards."

*

"It's twelve o'clock noon, you remembered to be home."

"Sure, I said I would. Where else would I be on a Sunday morning?"

"I wouldn't know. Maybe eating lunch on Nob Hill with your friends the hoi polloi."

She didn't mean hoi polloi; but if you roll that phrase around your tongue long enough it can acquire a deceptive taste of affluence.

"I don't have any hoi polloi friends. And the only time I'm on Nob Hill is in a worn-out tux behind an out-of-tune piano. How've you been?".

"I'll let you in on something, sonny. I'm going on 88 years old. I'm hanging on by a string and it better be strong."

"That's pretty good."

"Sure it is. How many people do you know going on 88?"

"I mean the image, hanging by a string..."

"I wish I could see images. I was watching, 'Gone With the Wind' on television last night. Gable was just a splotch, a body with ears, no face. I don't see faces any more unless they're on top of me, blown up."

"You took me to that movie when I was ten or so."

"I took you kids to a lot of movies."

In the early thirties, soon after my father died, she began shlepping Mark and me into town every Saturday afternoon, rain, shine, or snow. If there was a film with Gable or Herbert Marshall, her favorites, we might go twice in a week. We lived some two miles from the downtown theaters. In mid-winter she bundled us in scarves, mittens, hooded sweaters, and we trudged uphill to the trolley line on June Street. "But to try to save the thirty cents (total) fare while we were waiting, she'd prop Mark against a nearby tree, facing him in another direction as if he didn't belong to us, clutch my hand and stick her free thumb out, bold as any turnpike show girl. She didn't much look like one; but I was undersized and projected a waif-like air (I've been told), and invariably someone stopped. "Main Street, Loew's Poli Palace, or the Capitol on Franklin," she'd say—simultaneously motioning behind her back to Mark—as if we were entering a taxi and she was graciously offering the cabbie a choice of destinations.

"When I was still going to Leiberman's Market, never mind the meat, all I was seeing was bodies floating behind the counter. I said, Alex, if that's you—I can't see—I trust you. Give me a nice chuck roast. I don't go any more. I don't eat roasts. Your brother shops for me once, twice a week. What do I need, Campbell's soup, a few vegetables, some pieces of chicken. Never mind. Tell me about you. You got enough money? You don't regret giving up in Rhode Island?"

In 1949, holding a B.A. degree in organic chemistry, I took a job in a soap factory in Pawtucket, Rhode Island for fifty dollars a week. The company manufactured a line of industrial detergents.

To my final breath I will not forget the aroma of a primary
ingredient used in one of the syntheses. Benzyl mercaptan was its
odious name—a vile and insidious sulfur-based oil that clogged the
nostrils, permeated the pores. For months I had entire lunch
counters to myself; bus seats adjacent, fore, and aft were vacated
with alacrity. Rigorous scrubbings with the harshest of laundry
soaps could not eradicate it, nor could the most stringent of
colognes mask it. I fought Mr. Mercaptan for six stinking months
before jumping ship; swam to shore, crawled off into the brush
and never looked back.

"I would've made a lousy chemist, Ma."

"That's something you'll never know. How's Paula? You never
put her on the phone."

"Paula's fine." At least she ought to be, considering the house,
the car, the furniture I laid on her. "She's not here now."

Paula and I split three years ago; I never got around to telling
her. My brother's wife Naomi had died a few weeks earlier, and it
seemed like too much *tsuris* to put on her in such a short time.
Now it's too late.

"You give her my love."

"I will...Well, this is running long. We don't want to make
AT and T rich."

"Don't be a *nudzh*, I'm the one paying."

"Like I said before, I'll be more than happy to split the bill with
you. Right down the middle or even a slice to the side."

"Save your money—go buy yourself a new tuxedo. I'll call next
Sunday, same time, same station."

"Okay. Meanwhile hang in there."

"Sure I'll hang in there. What else have I got to do? I'll hang in there till someone taps me on the shoulder and like your friend Vivien Leigh says, I'll be poofff, gone with the wind."

I hang up a few moments later, racking my brain. Did Leigh ever use the title in dialogue or soliloquy? Did anyone?

*

"It's high noon, sonny, and all's well."

"Hi there. How you doing?"

"How'm I doing? I'll give you another image. Last year I was holding on, this year I'm hanging on."

"Not too shabby."

"Jay piled in here with his gang last night. We watched the ball game."

"Why doesn't he watch at his place?"

"He comes every night at six to see me. If there's a game on and he's got a bet with Sid or Louie, or the one with the nickname that sounds like a gangster, Harriet's boy—"

"Blackie?"

"—Blackie, they tag along. They pour the whiskey shots, nosh on the cheese and crackers, I watch the game with them. What I can see of it. People in white suits, ghosts running around on green. The contrasts I can make out. Between innings we *shmooz* a little, what can I tell you. . ."

I picture her on the sofa between these heavy-betting, hard-drinking baseball freaks, men in their late fifties and sixties—their mothers, her former friends and canasta partners, all gone now—

reacting to the whirl of emotions in the room, exhortations, curses, holding up her end of the banter ("A triple only? Couldn't he stretch it?"—Mark tells me she's got the jargon down pretty damn good); trying to be one of the gang, a good trouper.

"The smell of whiskey always bothered you."

"It's too late for that. The cigars are worse. Blackie used to light one up after another, now he's more careful with me. I tell him, Blackie, you want to smoke a cigar, go ahead, it's your lungs. He says, Sophie, you're a *mensh*. But he keeps it down to one and sits across the room from me. If it's a warm night he'll blow it out the window."

"How does Mark do? Does he win more than he loses?"

"I think the other way around. Some nights he loses his shirt, he gets mad. I tell him, If you want to throw your money away, go ahead, you earned it. They make bets on the side, if the hitter's going to take a walk or someone's going to run into a double play . . ."

"Can you really get interested in all that?"

"You'd be surprised how you can *make* yourself interested. I told myself years ago, Don't let yourself get old, keep pushing. . . Your brother's very good to me, he takes care of everything. . . He keeps his eye on me. If I'm walking across the room to the stairs or the kitchen—I call it walking, some people would say it's more like baby steps—and I come too close to a chair, a table corner, he'll say, Watch it! I tell him, How can I watch it if I can't see it!" She laughs, a dry roupy sound. "But he doesn't say much to me about himself. Financially I know he's all right but. . . When you

talk to him does he sound lonely? Does he ever talk about Naomi?"

"Once in a while. But I think he's pretty much over that."

"He still keeps all her clothes in the closets, her furs and dresses and shoes, the bedroom closed up. Dr. Fine, Harry, did the same thing when Lenore passed on. I see Harry now and then when something goes wrong. You remember his sister Edie? She never married, she used to take you kids to Easton's for ice cream sundaes..."

"A tall lady. She had a scratchy voice—I used to think of ground glass—and she wore her glasses on a ribbon."

"That's Edie. Harry had to put her in a nursing home last month. Eighty-two. She lost a few marbles. All my friends— they're either gone or off to Halifax."

I remember that locution from childhood. I'd hear her on the phone: So-and-so's off to Halifax. *Meshugga,* crazy.

"And you keep rolling along. You're the Mississippi River of the west side."

"Well, I got all my marbles, but physically don't ask me."

"What sort of things go wrong?"

"I'm not...speak louder."

"You said you see Harry Fine when something goes wrong. Like what?"

"A backache, the digestion; sometimes a sore throat won't go away. When you're 87 you get...uneasy. Your brother takes me to see Harry. He patches me up, slaps me on the you-know-what. Plenty miles in the old girl yet, he says. The last time we talked

about his sister—now they've salted her away. Poor Edie, she's begun another life. Soon will come the tap on the shoulder."

"You used that expression before."

"Tap on the shoulder? Don't you remember the story about your grandfather Julius and the Angel of Death in his dream?"

"No."

"I must have told you, you forgot. You remember how hard he was of hearing? . . ."

"We'd yell at him and he'd say, Don't holler, I can hear—but he couldn't."

"From 65 on he didn't hear two words. He wouldn't use the hearing aid, it made a buzz in his ear, he said. The salesman came twice and went away a beaten man."

"He went to a movie almost every afternoon. If one was held over he'd see it twice. When I asked him how the show was he'd say, Too talky, no—*Too much talk*. But half the time he wouldn't understand me and he'd answer, The fish was fine but the soup was too cold, or Stop *kvetching,* I took a bath this morning."

"That's it, with some things your memory's good. The last few years when he was at the Home he started having the same dream. I visited two, three times a week and he'd tell me about it. The Angel of Death would appear suddenly behind a door or on a street corner and tap him on the shoulder and say, Are you ready to come with me, Julius? I'm sorry, I don't hear you, he'd say. Next night the same thing. I still don't hear you, and the Angel would go away. But in his 91st year just a month before he passed on I visited him and he was . . . not suffering but he'd had enough. He

wasn't sleeping good, his dreams were...different. He said to me, You know if I ever have that dream again and the Angel taps me on the shoulder, I'll tell him, Don't holler, I can hear."

"Ah..."

"You're not laughing."

"It's funny—not that kind of funny. There seems to be, uh, quite a lot of—"

"I'm not getting you. Clear your throat."

"There's a lot of longevity in the family."

"But we're coming down to the end of the line. You kids didn't produce."

*

"Hi, Ma."

"Mark? How did you know it was me?"

"It's Sunday, twelve bells. You're always on the button."

"Wait a minute, there's a racket. I have to close the window..."
A good two minutes pass. "It's Nathan next door. A new family, they moved in last month. He rollerskates around the house."

"Does he bother you?"

"He's a little devil. When I drop a dish and break it—it happens a lot now—if the windows are open I hear him yell."

"Yell what?"

"Something hits again—ladyfingers."

"Butterfingers strikes again?"

"That's it—the exact words."

"I'll give him a kick in the *tuchis*."

"Where, from California? You and Paula better think about coming for a visit, I'm not getting any younger."

She's right, I'm long overdue for a trip back, but there are extenuating factors. (1) I have a steady gig playing vintage standards in a class continental restaurant. Such jobs are at a premium; a lot of my contemporaries are scuffling. If you don't own a rock-disco repertoire today—most musicians of my era not only don't own one, they have vowed to cut their throats before letting one in the house—you get used to eating sparingly. If I split for even a week I fear my position will be in jeopardy. A pianist a hair better (or someone management *thinks* is a hair better), a few years younger, an iota more charming, would be prowling home base, badmouthing my replacement (hand-picked for his bare-minimum competency); I wouldn't have to cut my throat, someone would do it for me. (2) I have a legitimate fear of flying. The last time I boarded a plane was in the spring of '74; San Francisco to Chicago, a visit with my in-laws. As we were approaching Denver the pilot announced he was turning back. Something about a loose door latch. Three weeks later a Turkish Airlines DC-10 crashed in a forest outside Paris with 346 aboard. No survivors. Three hundred and forty-six. They blamed it on a cargo door that didn't close properly. It gives you pause, makes you step to the side and consider. (3) I have no money. The cost of living in this town is horrendous. (Mark has the bread in the family, having wisely deserted the test tube-ad-beaker trenches for a behind-the-lines sales post.) Everything went to Paula—one of those unanticipated bloodbaths; people don't get clobbered like

that any more. But I'm not complaining: I can still read without a magnifying glass, phone without counting holes in a dial; my furniture, what there is of it, is comfortably dispersed about my two snug rooms.

". . . Your cousin Natalie came by to see me. You used to baby-sit for her, remember?"

"Sure, she was a cute kid. Long brown hair, dimples. . ."

"She just got divorced from a *shaygets* in Fall River. She came over Friday with her mother, your aunt Lilian. She went up like a balloon—225 pounds."

"Natalie?"

"I squeezed it out of Lil on the phone yesterday. That makes her more than two of me. She filled the room—like one of those balloons over Macy's on Thanksgiving. I didn't see the face, just the body, that was enough."

"The kid ain't so cute any more."

" 'You must have been a beautiful baby,' " my mother is singing in a frail rasping voice, " 'but baby look at you now. . .' We used to play duets on that song the year you were taking lessons with Mrs. Wheeler, remember? And the other one—'Are you having any fun, are you doing any liiiv-ing?. . .' " The voice trembles and croaks like one of those sleepy frogs I'd hear summer afternoons in the rushes of Lake Quinsigamond.

"I think you got that second line wrong, Ma. It's 'What you gettin' out of liiiv-in'?. . .' " Raised in tenuous song, my voice quavers and cracks like an asthmatic schoolboy's.

"I won't argue with you, you're the piano player. She used to love my lemon meringue pies."

"Natalie? Well, they were terrific." It's true. Those pies—she
bungled every other dessert she attempted, I won't even mention
entrees—were famed throughout Worcester's Jewish west side, a
small but discriminating community. On her 70th birthday my
brother had proposed a toast at a large family gathering; he'd been
eloquent and funny and a little smashed. The toast, written out
beforehand and committed to memory, ran approximately:
"Revered wife and mother, devoted helpmeet, dishclearer, house-
cleaner, undercooker of carrots, burner of innumerable pot roasts,
baker of magnificent lemon meringue pies..." at which point a
younger member of the clan (it must have been Natalie) cried out,
"That divine meringue, the snowy peaks of Everest!" Distracted,
Mark lost momentum and ran off the tracks. Tried to recover,
floundered, blew it again; took a memory-refreshing slug of
bourbon, spluttered, gagged, and doubled over in a paroxysm of
coughing. "Now the other one," my mother said as a strapping
nephew pounded him on the back. "The whole family's turning
into drunkards."

"'...Before you're old and grey, still okay—'" She's back in
Tunesville 1939 ("Are You Having Any Fun?"), having skipped
the bridge, taking the last eight out with tag—"'have a little fun,
son, have a little fun...'" Maybe this is it, I speculate, that which
sooner or later comes to us all: the dreaded loss of marbles.
Mercifully she stops. "When I got mad at you kids I used to sing to
control my temper."

"I don't remember that."

"When I started singing you and Jay knew I meant business.
Now I can't sing any more, the vocal chords have dried up. It's all
right, I can do without it. There's no one to get mad at any more."

"But you're feeling okay in general?"

"I sleep more in the daytime now. I fall asleep in my favorite chair, the rose-colored one—that's my indoor sport these days. At night as soon as my head hits the pillow I'm wide awake. Everything considered, I'm not doing bad. But it's becoming a battle, it's more downhill than up now. I don't know what else to tell you. The battle's on and I'm holding the fort."

*

She hit 88 (I thought of keys on the piano and the big blizzard—the year she was born), then 90 (-year wonder, a cat's life times 10), then 92 (in the shade, movin' on up there) and she kept on going.

*

"Top o' the morning to you, Ma."

"You knew it was me."

"It's twelve o'clock high, isn't it?"

"I almost missed the time, I snoozed off. I used the operator this time, I've been spinning wrong numbers. I said to her, I'm sorry to bother you but I'm 93 years old. She said, It's no bother and God bless you. Everybody's saying that to me lately, so I feel blessed."

"Did you get my letter last week?" I had written three pages in block letters an inch high.

"I heard about it. Don't send me any more letters, I can't read them. I don't like to ask your brother to read extra to me, he does enough."

"Not even with the glass?"

"I don't use it any more, it's too much bother. My hand shakes. I can use the left to hold the right hand still but who's going to hold the left?"

"I get the picture."

"The last couple weeks Nathan has been out on the front stoop afternoons when I go get the mail. Sometimes I can't find it all in the box or I scratch my hand on the metal. He hands it to me. Yesterday I said to him, Nathan, you're a *mensh*, why are you so good to me. Know what he said?"

"Tell me."

"Because you're so old."

"How old's this Nathan now?"

"Must be thirteen, fourteen."

"Has the kid got all his marbles?"

"At that age he better have. He pushes the letters at me, they're mostly dividend checks. I don't see his hand. I don't see faces or bodies any more, only outlines. I can tell colors— something light on the green carpet underneath me. If I drop a Kleenex or a paper I can find it. There's a gold chair across the room. A new covering—you wouldn't know, you haven't been here. I see it against the green, light on dark, a contrast. The new eye man Weinglass said, I can't do anything more for you, Sophie, but you'll always see contrasts. Sophie he calls me. Two visits and already we're on intimate terms."

"What about trees? You still take walks, don't you?"

"Well, like I said I see the outlines. Especially in summer when the leaves are thick. Sure, I still walk. If it's good weather—not too

hot or too cold, in between—I take a little spin around the house
with my walking cane. Some people would say more like a shuffle
than a spin. It takes me fifteen minutes, one circle. At night in
warm weather I sit out on the back porch. I can see sunsets, the
moon against a black sky...what I call the vivid contrasts. I can
see some stars if they're bright and sparkly enough, what can I tell
you..."

"You're telling me a lot."

"I eat with my fingers now, I don't trust the fork and knife. I
eat soup and things I can lift in my hands. Tuna fish, cooked
vegetables, some pieces of chicken. It gets a little sloppy. Last week
your cousin Natalie the balloon came with her granddaughter
while I was eating—"

"Natalie has a *granddaughter?*"

"Sure, you forget how time flies, sonny, it goes like the wind. I
was having an early lunch. I didn't know they were coming, so I
kept on eating. When I get hungry I get hungry. The girl—I can't
think of her name—she's bright as a button. She must have been
watching me. That's how people eat in Hawaii, she said.
Afterward I always have a cup of hot water. I heat the pan, I can
see when it gets red it must be boiling. I turn off the stove and
walk away from it—"

"You sure you should be using a stove?"

"I'm careful, I walk away till the red fades, then I come back.
Your brother wants to bring someone in to cook and help out,
four, six hours a day. He already has someone once a week to
clean. I told him, Not on your life, I'm not losing any more of my
privacy. I told you boys a long time ago I never want to be a

burden on you. I've seen how parents can be a pain in the neck—
kids who would've been better off orphans. If your brother had
asked me to come live with him while Naomi was here I would've
refused him, point blank. Now he knows better...Oh, that's what
I wanted to tell you. Remember your Aunt Seal?"

"Sure, Dad's youngest sister. You're not going to tell me
she's—"

"No, Daisy was the youngest, Seal next. She called me twice in
August from Springfield to wish me a happy birthday. It made me
so sad..."

"Why? What's another birthday?"

"She called me twice in the same week. She forgot she called
the first time. I figure she's losing some marbles. Two Saturdays
ago, sure enough, the daughter Mimi and her husband took her to
a nursing home. The boy, Ted, you remember died in the war.
Poor Seal, she's started another life."

Another good trouper shipped out to Halifax. "Seal was one of
your steady canasta players. When I'd come home afternoons from
May Street—"

"It was mah-jong, canasta hadn't come in yet."

"Anyway when I got home from school on Wednesdays there'd
be four of you at the card table with the coffee and cakes, and a
fifth kind of floating around the action. You had the best china out
and someone was always smoking like a stove—"

"Lena Altschul. It was Tuesday, not Wednesday."

"You played for money. I used to worry you were losing and we
wouldn't be able to go to the movies that week. I'd come in the

back door through the hallway and try to sneak up to my room,
but Seal would always trap me and make me play for her."

"'My Blue Heaven,' that was the song she always asked for. You
played it good with a bouncy left hand. Lena would applaud and
call Encore!, squinting with the cigarette in her mouth."

"How do you remember details like that?"

"I remember everything way back, it's what happened an hour
and a half ago I forget. 'My Blue Heaven,' that was Seal's favorite.
She probably still sings it unless the voice is dried up like mine...
'When whippoorwills call, and evening is nigh...'" she sings, or
what passes for it; the feeble croak has become a tremolo wheeze,
a cracked whisper. "I was thinking the other day of that first
nightclub you played at, Aunt Jenny's Café. You tried to hide it
from me you were just a kid..."

"Jan's Waterfont Café."

"That's it. Up near Harrington Corner."

"I guess Allie told you." A ramshackle dive high and dry on the
Pleasant Street hill (belying its name) two miles from any water:
stranded like the ark on Mt. Ararat. At the time of my residency
during the early forties it was a soldier-and-sailor hangout, and our
fledgling piano-trumpet-drums combo, the Tunesmiths, operated
in constant jeopardy from liquid-propelled missiles—flying beer
bottles. She never knew how raunchy those wartime gutbuckets
were, and if my father had been living I would never have served
my apprenticeship, much less been allowed to stay the course; to
this day I'd be juggling test tubes in some malodorous soap factory
or other, driving bus passengers from their seats, emptying lunch

counters. When I left the house evenings I'd tell her I was working a country-club dinner party, a church social or synagogue dance. But her brother-in-law Allie found out about Jan's. He dropped in one night when a goodly brawl was under way, navy blue- and khaki-clad bodies ricocheting off booths, *nafkas* shrieking, and white-helmeted whistle-blowing MPs beginning to pile in with raised batons—in the teeth of which the Tunesmiths launched chorus after chorus of the "Star Spangled Banner" with as much effect on the combatants as a bird call in a blizzard. Uncle Allie, ashen-faced, cowered just inside the doorway; I saw a bottle of Pickwick Ale (the label as distinctive as an aircraft's markings) sail inches past his head and bang off the wall. "I won't tell your mother about this," he said after the smoke had cleared and the MPs were herding bloodied servicemen into the paddy wagons. "It would see her to an early grave. But if you're serious about pursuing this vocation I suggest you come to my office first thing Monday morning and we'll see about taking out a substantial policy on your life."

". . . You used to come home smelling like a brewery."

"I wasn't drinking all that much, though. The smoke and fumes would get in my clothes."

"So you come home every night to Paula with the smoke and the fumes?"

"Uh-uh. I play only class joints these days, Ma."

"But it's just pushing keys up and down. You sure you don't have any regrets about giving up Rhode Island?"

"Not a one. You know what's always amazed me," I say, to nudge her off the track. "How well you hear. I mean, a few things may be fading but your hearing's terrific."

"Well, some voices are better than others. High voices, women,
I hear better. You always had a high voice."

". . . Funny, I don't hear it myself."

"It's high. A little like a woman."

"Uh-huh. So outside the eyes you're feeling up to snuff?"

"I'll put it to you this way, sonny. The fort's crumbling but the
flag's still flying."

I used to wonder if she'd culled a ghost writer from the legions
of bright nieces and nephews who dropped by to visit when they
came through town, but Mark assured me that the metaphors,
though not necessarily extemporaneous, were hers. No question
the quality of the one-liners has been improving, mellowing with
age like wines and violins. The fort-flag image is at the heart of
her more inspired efforts. Last month she came up with the rather
pedestrian "I used to swing and sway, now I only sway," and prior
to that, "I'll be shuffling off any year now but it won't be to
Buffalo" (resurrecting another hoary duet on the old Story & Clark
upright—one of our last performances, for soon afterward she'd
closed the song book permanently, saying I was getting too good
for her and she didn't want to cramp my style). Occasionally her
replies are direct and unadorned: "How am I feeling? Sonny, I'm
93 years old, and 93 is 93 no matter how you slice it."

"You know what keeps me going?" she says now. "Up and
down the stairs to the bedroom, five, six times a day. Harry Fine
says it's probably why I'm still here. But I'll let you in on
something. It's easier walking up and down than level."

"Why should that be?"

"Well, think about it."

"Easier up and down. . .doesn't make sense. Down maybe. I give up."

"I have the bannister for support. Across the room I move like a baby afraid of falling. I kind of just shuffle along. . ." Her voice takes on a lilt and for a moment I fear she is going to break into a chorus of the old Buffalo floor-thumper. "Harry says there's a few miles left in old Dobbin but I don't know, it gets harder. I have to keep pushing. . ."

"Speaking of up and down I see your stocks are going pretty good. American T and T is the highest it's been in years. Maybe you ought to consider selling." To my everlasting shame I confess I've been following, with more than casual interest, the vacillations of her blue chips.

"I used to follow the prices every day, wait for the dividend checks. Now I can't be bothered—never mind bothered, there's nothing to see. I let Jay do all that. He collects the dividends, signs, puts everything in the bank for me. From here on down to the end of the line I'm Mickey the dunce. Just let the AT and T sit there. At 93 I can't worry about buying or selling. When I close my eyes it isn't going to make any difference. I'll go out the way I came in, without American Telephone and Telegraph."

*

"Hello?"

"Sunday high noon, sonny, just like the movie..."

But it isn't Sunday, it's Saturday. The first slip. Her voice is different, it's paper-thin and phlegm-clotted; it cracks to pieces as it does when she tries to sing. It sounds like everything I've ever

heard about decline and deterioration, a voice just past the bend in the road, the far side of Halifax.

"Hi. How're you doing?"

"How'm I doing? Well, the old mare's still standing but she ain't doing much kicking..." She clears her throat. "I was listening to television this morning. I heard your friend Mae West died."

This is an old routine of hers (familiarity where none exists) that hasn't been out of the mothballs much in recent years: I see where your friend Harry Truman got mad at a reporter. I hear your old pal Elizabeth Taylor's getting married again. "Someone mentioned it to me last night. How old was she?" I ask, and wish I hadn't.

"Eighty-eight years. A spring chicken."

"Practically a babe in arms."

"How's your weather out there?..."

The voice is coming apart, dissolving in its own juices. Its timbre reminds me of my Uncle Morris, her oldest brother. Into his middle-sixties he had been a dapper urbane man with a resonant voice and matinee-idol good looks. By the time he died at 76 the voice had become a dry husk. Near the end I remember complimenting him on a handsome silk sport shirt he was wearing. "I can't wear ties any more, I can't wear collars," he said in a hoarse whisper. "I have no neck left."

"The weather? It's like it always is in San Francisco—fifty-eight degrees and overcast. How's it back there?"

"It's snowing. Someone phoned earlier and told me not to go out. They didn't have to phone, I haven't been out of the house in two months. I look out—all I see is a glare. I can't tell snow from

rain. The cataracts are thick now. When you come for a visit, if you get around to it, I want you to be prepared for my eyes. They're a different color. . ."

I try to remember their color and fail.

". . .I know I can't ask for anything to work again, but it's all right. I'm meeting it as I should. I understand about blind people, how they're able to do it. My heart is out to them. But Jay—Mark, I'll be truthful, if I didn't keep pushing hard all the time now I'd fall flat on my face. I'm beginning to feel. . .apprehensive."

Such a precise unexpected word: as if a young child were to say, I'm feeling. . .melancholy. The turn of mood on this somber fall day has caught me off balance; I ask uneasily, mindlessly, "Why apprehensive?"

"I don't want you to misunderstand me, there's no sadness. Sure, I would've liked to dance a few more dances at the ball— that's an expression your father used to use. But if the Angel were to tap me now and say, You're coming with me tonight, or tomorrow, I'd take it in stride. I just don't want anything else to go wrong. I can't look out and see what's going on, so it's a little frightening. I'm sensitive to everything that isn't right, or is wrong. The days are. . .fizzing away. I'm just thankful for each one now. I don't have a past or future, only the present—just like a child. That's my approach to. . .to a method of living. I want you boys to realize I'll say good night soon. I have you both, you and Jay, Mark and you. Your brother I have every day, you on the phone once every week. It's more than enough. I love you both very much. Don't misunderstand, I'm not being sad. I'm meeting this in the way I should. But I'll tell you the real truth, the only

reason I go on pushing is to be with you kids a while longer, that's it in a nutshell. . . ."

This has taken long minutes: the slow deliberate cadence that is like a threnody, marked by frequent throat-clearing.

"Ma," I have to clear my own throat, "there's no way you should be alone any more."

"There's some furniture Paula would love to have when I close my eyes. An onyx table beside the gold chair, I'm sitting there now. You wouldn't remember, you haven't been in so long. I can feel it with my hands, it's. . .grained, solid. People comment over it. And the Limoges china in the cabinet I haven't used probably since the last canasta game. . .I already discussed it with your brother, I want cremation. If you want to mail a few seeds to Israel, plant a small tree like the kids did for Morris I wouldn't be unhappy. That's my memorial. . . ."

The frail voice is ruptured, doomed. "Hey, you got some time left," I blurt, my thoughts careening. Memorial: *Baker of magnificent lemon meringue pies, undercooker of carrots* . . . You'd go at them with a fork and they'd bounce off the plate like Mexican jumping beans. Uncle Allie used to say, Those carrots were what drove your father to an early grave. "Ma, when those seeds are planted, a lot of years from now, a sturdy oak will grow."

"Oh, sure." Her laugh is like a whippoorwill's cough. "Well, it's a nice thought. You say hello to Paula. Why doesn't she ever come on the phone? Doesn't she like me?"

"She adores you. I think I told you she usually lunches with friends on Saturdays—Sundays. But she always asks after you."

"So maybe we should change the time."

"No, keep it. We're grooved into it."

"*Vuss?* Now I don't hear..."

"We're grooved, locked into it. You and me. Twelve o'clock high, our time." I suddenly feel like a singsong idiot.

"I'm going to put down the phone and take a snooze now. I sleep a lot in the day. Today I'm—If you noticed something funny in my throat I caught a little cold yesterday."

"Ah...So what're you doing for it?"

"The aspirin and Vick's Vapor-Rub, same as I used to give you kids. If it goes on too long your brother picks me up, we go see Harry. He gives me pills. Heavy-duty stuff like for horses, he says."

"So outside of the cold you're feeling okay?" I ask, hoping for a zinger, a vintage one-liner to brush away the strands of the shroud that have been woven this grey November noontime.

"Mark dear, I'm 94 years old. I'll let you slice that any way you want from here till the buggy ride is over."

*

A few months later my brother phoned from Worcester in the early morning. She had fallen out of bed during the night and injured her hip. She'd lain on the floor for hours and waited until dawn to pull the phone off the bed table and call him. "She didn't want to wake me!" He phoned for an ambulance and rushed over. "She's at Doctor's Hospital. The hip is bruised, but she's okay."

"Only bruised? Amazing." I'd heard about elderly people's hips—never mind elderly in this case: ancient. The joints lose

bone density, crack like peanut shells and are never the same again.

"Fine says it's a miracle there was no fracture. They'll keep her a day or two for observation. But this is it. She can't live alone any more."

"Agreed."

"I'm going to start interviewing people. Her privacy is out the window. You know the real reason she doesn't want anyone living with her, don't you?"

"So the money she's saving for us doesn't drain away."

"Exactly. I told her, Relax, it's on me. She won't listen. It's like that story about her father and the angel: Sorry, I don't hear you. You know, I've been carrying the brunt here. You ought to come back, see what I've been going through."

"I can imagine. I don't have to tell you I appreciate it, Mark...Listen, one thing I never got straight—why didn't they do surgery on her eyes when the cataracts started? Was she too old?"

"I told you years ago. It was degeneration of the optic nerve *plus* cataracts. A double whammy. The old grey mare's wearing permanent blinders."

*

"I missed Sunday. I've been in the hospital."

"I know all about it. I tried to reach you. How's the hip?"

"I spin around the house a little slower is all. I was in the middle of a dream when it happened."

I hesitate to ask her the content. "I'm coming home, Ma, a little visit."

"Oh... You're taking the plane? You got enough money?"

"I got enough."

"Will Paula come?"

"I don't have that much."

"Your brother's after me about a live-in. Every day he *hoks* me..."

"He's absolutely right. We'll discuss it when I get there."

"So when are you coming?"

"I'm taking a red-eye flight Saturday night after work. Mark's picking me up in Boston. I'll be there Sunday."

"Don't talk to me about red eyes. Mine are a different color. I told you to be prepared for it. There are a couple other changes too."

"I'm prepared."

"I don't look like one of the Flora Dora girls any more."

"I look at your picture on my piano every day. You were in your late twenties, a zaftig all-American beauty queen."

"Well, outside the weight I wasn't too bad in those days."

"Something I always meant to ask. How come you never got married again? You were in your prime. There must have been an offer or two..."

"Oh, I had my hands full with you kids. As I look back... it was too much trouble. There was one fellow—but he was poor and had a boy and girl of his own. I didn't want someone who would boss you and Jay around. Your father was a brilliant witty man, you were too young to remember. He wasn't what you'd call good-look-

ing, but he was. . .to the manner born and had this terrific wit.
When he and Sam Behrman got together at dinner parties it was
like—like Shakespeare and Bernard Baruch. People hung on every
word. So afterward I kept my eye out for a brilliant witty man who
looked like Clark Gable. You try to find one around Worcester. But
that's all water under the dam. Oh—it's going to be so good seeing
you. . ."

"It'll be good to see you, too. Everything okay otherwise?"

"I got a tooth needs capping. The dentist wanted to pull it but
for once I decided I won't be stingy. I said, Milton, nothing doing,
you cap it. It would be expensive, he said. I said, I can barely chew
the boiled chicken as it is. Cap it. I know what's on his mind. I may
be Mickey the dunce when it comes to vision and a couple other
things, but most of the marbles are still there. He thinks, Why
cap? She'll be gone in two months, next week."

*

"Here he is, signed, sealed and delivered," Mark says.

I recognize her and I don't. She's doll-sized incredibly shrunken;
what little flesh there is is pendulous, the face is deeply scored. She
looks 95 no matter how you slice it.

"Hi, Ma, I'm here."

"Oh." The desiccated arms grope, establish contact, encircle my
waist; the top of her head comes to my breastbone and I'm short,
five-feet six. "You lost weight, the last time I couldn't reach around
you so easy."

"Maybe your arms grew," Mark shouts at her cheerfully and immediately switches on the tube, an NFL game from Miami.

She toddles across the green carpet to the pale gold chair, tugging me by the hand; feels for the chair arms, pivots with slow evenly-spaced steps and cranks herself down, an ancient doll on a gilded throne. The traversal of the small room and the settling in have taken long minutes. "There's a stool against the wall that goes with the chair," she says. "Pull it over for yourself. Sit close." The voice is feeble, trembling over a half-octave range, a loosely strung violin; less sure than it was on the phone only days ago.

I squat before her on the matching stool; alongside her chair is the milky-green onyx table she spoke of, holding a dial telephone and a small vase of silk flowers. Gazing into the hooded unseeing eyes, the corrugate graven face, I feel I am at the feet of some snowy-haired tribal matriarch, a venerable seeress, a noble (crumbling) fort. She leans forward, reaches for my hand; a thin smile flickers at the corners of the parched mouth. "Well, do I look 95 to you?"

I must be kind, or witty. I appropriate the stock reply of a fiftyish lecher friend of mine when asked his age by young girls: "I'm closer to 40, baby, than to 30."

"I'd say you look closer to 85 than to 75."

"What?"

"You have to yell," Mark says over the television sound.

I repeat the line, which doesn't sound so great the second time; I don't think she hears it. Maybe if I raised the pitch of my voice. . . more of a woman's intonation.

"Look at my eyes," she says.

They have a bluish silvery cast. "What about them?"

"What color are they?"

"Blue."

"What?"

"Blue."

"What color did they used to be?"

I've tried to remember and still can't. I take an informed guess: "Brown." Same as mine.

"Brown," she confirms. "The blue is the cataracts, the glare."

We talk about this and that: weather, Paula, doctors, relatives, stocks and bonds, old songs—what we've been talking about for eight years on the phone. I have to repeat most everything at least twice, loudly, over the low rumble of the football game, and after half an hour I'm hoarse. Less than a week ago she heard me so clearly. I notice that whenever I speak her lips move—she's silently mouthing my words a fraction of a beat behind. Mark's eyes are riveted on the screen, a hand folded across his mouth; he hasn't spoken more than two dozen words. Self-preservation.

The eyelids droop and close. She's dropping off, her right hand threaded lightly across her mouth—and this familial gesture, an adjunct of pensiveness, comes back to me. It's here now in this room, mother and oldest son, and I link it to various aunts and uncles and grandparents over the decades in memory and in faded sepia snapshots.

I join Mark on the sofa, my legs cramped from the forced crouch, the constant leaning forward. The house looks tiny to me, the three downstairs rooms matchbox-sized; maybe it has to do with the furniture pushed against the walls. I can't believe the

three of us lived under this roof for fifteen-some years without physical and spiritual abrasion. The miniature figure across the way, though dwarfed by the big chair, has a strangely commanding presence. With her head leaned back in deep repose, speckled papery hads now extended on the chair arms, sunken eyes closed, she takes on a timeless, almost Biblical cast, the gaunt wasted face an archaic mask. She could be the mother of Abraham.

The Dolphins score and Mark curses, slams the arm of the sofa; he has 75 bucks riding on the Broncos.

"What do you think she's thinking?" I ask him.

There's a delicate throat-clearing sound across the room. "My mind's a total blank," she says evenly.

I stare at Mark; he shrugs. "Sometimes the words slip through."

"The three of us—" her voice deserts her—"we haven't been in this room together in a long time. . ." The head sinks back into the gold, and I begin to understand the energy she must have hoarded for those weekly phone calls.

It's half-time: we're watching a hundred high-school girls high-stepping in glitter corselets when the phone rings.

She comes forward with a little start, gropes for the receiver on the table, lifts it. A small light on the casing goes on. "Hello?. . . Frieda, hold on a minute. . ." I watch a trembling finger move to a gadget above the dial. "Okay, dear, talk to me. How are you feeling?. . ." Of course: the volume control on an amplifying device. Had a residue of vanity made her conceal it from me all these years? I see her lips move as Frieda's high-pitched chatter crackles over the line.

"How long has she been doing that—mouthing words as she listens?"

"Forever. Oh Jesus, look at this poor dolly..." One of the high-school girls has dropped her baton coming off the field; each time she tries to retrieve it she kicks it farther away; the camera fixes on her like blood on sand. "If there're any firearms around she'll shoot herself when she gets home," Mark says. Finally she drops to her knees near the sideline, head drooping in mortification; the announcer chuckles as the camera pans away.

The teams come on for the second half. Frieda is off the line, my mother's head is leaned back once again in timeless repose, eyes shut, twig-fingers splayed across her mouth. On the first play from scrimmage Miami intercepts. Mark comes halfway to his feet, pounding the sofa arm. "Stop him—stop the son of a bitch!" My mother doesn't move a muscle; she's either inured or doesn't hear. "Well, the goddam game's beyond redemption." He gets up, plods through the dining room to the john off the kitchen.

My mother's eyes come open. She clears her throat and begins to hoist herself out of the chair; it's a laborious process, craning forward, grasping the chair arms, boosting herself up by stages. In her sandals and white socks she shuffles across the carpet toward me with a smile slipped to one side of her face that's surprisingly sly—and familiar: it's the crafty, tart great-aunt smile Edward Everett Horton used to wear on mischievous occasions. She stops a few feet from me and addresses the corner of the sofa which Mark has vacated. "So you're losing your shirt again?"

Mark, returning from the john, lets loose a har-de-har laugh. "When I'm wearing dark clothes against the sofa there's no contrast—no way she can see me."

She turns in puzzlement at the sound of his voice, the silvery eyes agape, blinking.

"If you kids are making fun of me," she says in a wavering voice, and the foxy half-smile slowly reappears, "I got news for you. I couldn't care less."

*

I stay with Mark that night—sleeping in Naomi's bed ("It's time I did this," he says, and with an intake of breath tenderly pulls down the braided orange spread, its first removal since her death)—and spend the next two days with my mother while he's at work. At his suggestion I've worn dark pants and a light colored sweater of his so she can fix me against the brown sofa and track me around the house.

He has been interviewing women from agencies and has almost settled on one. A compromise has been reached: Sophie has agreed to having someone come in for a few hours a day to read whatever mail there is and "maybe beef up the menu," as she puts it. The ice has been broken; he hopes soon to have a woman sleeping in. I'll contribute what I can.

It's an ordeal trying to converse; my voice gives out early in the day. When I ask her about a hearing aid she says it's too late to fool around with the things, they make a buzz in the ear, she can't be bothered. I wonder if she's actually tried one or is relying on her

father's experience a generation ago. She's aware of the strain on me and for the most part is content to sit in the gold chair or on the sofa beside me, listening to the television news (tuned *loud*), nodding off and on—if I weren't there she'd go upstairs to nap— while I read the paper and browse through some of the books in the narrow four-shelf case that go back to my childhood: *David Copperfield, The Wonder Book of Science, A Connecticut Yankee in King Arthur's Court* ... The top shelf is occupied solely by a silver-framed photograph of my father in a dark ill-fitting business suit and straw boater, the frame affixed to one of those oldfashioned pedestals that allows it to swing freely. She comes out of her sitting-up snooze periodically to ask me what time it is (ordinarily she'd dial the phone service), and every two hours or so she toddles into the kitchen to fix a snack.

"The digestive system doesn't work so good any more—-it can't handle big loads. So I eat a lot of small meals just like people with ulcers." Watching her open cans—a 7-ounce Bumblebee tuna takes three, four minutes—fill a pan with water, turn on the stove, pour a glass of milk "for the bones and teeth" (holding a finger inside the glass to catch the level), I recall her gastronomic glory days, devouring shrimp-and-cucumber salads, Nova Scotia lox, rump steak and overdone chuck roasts, the boiled lobsters that Mark would bring home Saturday nights ready to eat from Messier's Diner. For a couple of years there, while I was in junior high, she was packing it on. An impassioned noontime/early-evening exhortation echoes down the corridor of years: "If I don't get something in my stomach right away I'm going to pass out of the picture." I offer to help, fill the pan, pour the milk; she refuses.

"I don't like to rely on anybody, I know where everything is." I experience an advance twinge of compassion for the lady Mark is going to employ.

The phone rings several times a day. Frieda again, Itsy (Isabel), Clara...One or two of the names strike a chord: former mah-jong and/or canasta partners, junior stalwart survivors. Her finger adjusts the volume control to each speaker. "I can't talk long, Mark's here from California...(lips moving) Who?...That's what I said, the youngest—he blew in from San Francisco." The "blew" I take to be a language slip until it recurs in the next call with a little English on it.

On Tuesday the bright cool weather turns soft and hazy, a melting Indian-summer day, and I join her in a little spin around the house. As we move out the front door I notice for the first time that thin sections of sponge have been taped to the protruding metal jamb fixture on which she might tear her skin.

In a heavy cloth coat, walking cane in one hand and my arm in the other, she moves at an infinitesimal pace, slower than any toddler just risen from the crouch, without the infant's unpredictable lurches. A few crusts of soggy snow linger in the hedges bordering the yard. The air is dense and luminous, weighted with half-remembered fragrances I cannot name.

"I can't take the cold like I used to. I haven't been able to read a thermometer in ten years. I stick my nose out the window to see what's what."

Between these drawn-out warm-weather circuits of the house, the frequent snacks and snoozes, the television news and telephone calls, I can see how the days pass for her. A raw teenage

face peers out at us from a side window of the house next door: Nathan, I presume.

We're walking into dazzle, a low autumn-afternoon sun as ripe and lustrous as a harvest moon. I have to shield my eyes.

"That feels so nice," she says.

"What, the warmth?"

"The light, the sun on my face. I can just make it out—it's like the bulb behind the bathroom door we had in the first house on Lovell Street. You remember, it was frosted glass."

I have a 7:30 flight out of Boston this evening. Mark has gone to Hartford on business, and I've rented a car for the drive to Logan Airport. At the open door the withered arms circle my waist again and I kiss the top of her head.

"Take care of yourself. Keep the flag flying."

"Sure but it's at half-mast from here on." Her voice rises and trembles with embryo laughter. "You come back when you can."

"I promise."

"Better make it soon, sonny. Any day now it'll be gone with the wind time." Her wily off-center smile taunts the prediction.

I push open the screen door—wondering why it's still in place in mid-November—and with a surprising deftness she reaches out and pulls it shut; it seems more reflex than a deliberate prolonging of departure.

"So it's going all right with you and Paula?"

"Sure, everything's fine." But I can tell by a slight lift of inflection, the set of her lips immediately afterward, that she knows; not everything, but she knows.

"And you're happy with your life now?"

"Absolutely."

"I once asked you if you had a million dollars would you do anything different. You said no."

"I don't remember that."

"How can you forget a million-dollar question?" She reaches blindly toward me for a last embrace. With my lips pressed against the sparse white hair I can feel her body quiver like a sparrow on a twig. She releases me. "Go catch your plane."

"That's not something I'm looking forward to."

"Believe me, there're worse things to be afraid of." She tries to smile. The light in the silver-blue eyes is smeared, a flat gleam, and the furrowed skin beneath is moist.

"I love you, Ma. Keep on pushin'."

"I'm doin' the best I can."

I walk out to the rented Dodge, get in. The car is facing the house. I see her framed in the doorway behind the screen, gazing sightlessly out, and think of her in another setting forty-odd years ago, framed in the yellow night light of the parlor window in the house on Lovell Street, keeping vigil, waiting for me to return from Jan's Waterfront Café. Before turning on the ignition I check my Worcester city map for access to the Mass. Turnpike, which hadn't been built when I was last here. There are several options—via Auburn, Millbury, North Grafton. When I look up a few minutes later she's still standing there motionless, as if waiting for me to leave. The day's light is all but gone, the Dodge is black; she can't possibly see it. Other cars have been entering the small circular drive of this dead-end street and parking, or

starting up and leaving. She must have assumed one of them was mine. I raise my hand to tap the horn, change my mind. Perhaps she's merely basking in the last light of this Indian-summer afternoon, time on her hands, imagining remembered sun, the light-bulb behind the frosted glass, warming her wasted flesh. I check the state map for the Turnpike exit to Logan Airport; I've been told it's complicated. She's still there in the deepening twilight. Another car a few yards from me starts up, pulls away. Her right hand is threaded over her mouth now in that musing wistful gesture (that I will see on myself in my bathroom mirror three mornings from now, thoughts tumbling like November leaves).

I return the maps to the glove compartment and start the motor, whose sound she has heard only once before—this morning when I arrived. Yet it trips a response. Could she, like a family pet, recognize an engine's timbre? I have no idea. Nothing changes in her posture except for her right hand: the fingers lift hesitantly from her mouth, and from a wrist bent like the most fragile of flowers, flutter. It is the shy and tentative gesture of a little girl waving bye to a stranger she has only just met.

THE BARRIER

BY THE LATE 1940s I knew the blacks had something I was in dire need of, and I was young and intrepid and naive enough to go looking for it.

From 52nd to 140th Street the winds of change were blowing strong. The convulsions of black-rebellion music exploding out of the theaters and cafés of Harlem had startled white musicians, turned us around; the music was angry, blazing, ferocious —yet always under a tight edge of control. "It' s a rogue boat heading for the New World," a black Boston drummer told me, "and Bird and Diz are the navigators."

I'd become aware of a widening chasm separating the levels of rhythmic propulsion achieved by white and black musicians. The former' s playing was more even-keeled, linear, lacking the sudden dips and spurts, the coiled-spring tension-and-release and un-expected displacement of meter that sent the beat slamming and teetering down the tracks like a highballing express, generating

incredible excitement. I was convinced there was something basic and vital that came easily to them and hard to us. I'd noticed, too, that at integrated jam sessions blacks and whites tended to call different tunes. When I'd suggested "Have you Met Miss Jones?" at an after-hours club a black had scoffed goodnaturedly, "That's one of your white-boy tunes." A similar judgment was passed on Gershwin's "A Foggy Day." Blacks leaned toward tunes with relaxed, more fluid structures—"Willow Weep For Me," "Georgia on My Mind"—written as often by white as black composers. "Willow's more leisurely and doesn't sweat," a black bass player said, "you got time to climb inside it, feel its bones, poke your way around. Your average Caucasian tune is boxy, four-squared, forces you into corners."

Other blacks I talked to found the whole subject of racial-genetic orientation distasteful, awakening the old we-got-rhythm stereotypes and images of grinning darkies dancing for pennies on southern street corners. "All you got to remember when you're blowing," a black drummer told me, "is one simple thing: Rice Krispies. Snap, crackle, pop." A tenor sax player I worked with at a Worcester Turnpike club was at once more specific and expansive: "Dancing and singing and lovemaking and making music have no more to do with color than making mudpies or building snowmen. Music's color blind. Absolutely. Ofay players occasionally pull my sleeve, talkin' about their whiteness closing them off from certain secrets of the trade. Listen to me: *they're ain't no secrets*. We all came out of the same alley. How you play has to do with who you listened to when you were coming up, who you hung out with and picked up on. Gershwin picked up on

the Harlem rent-party players and wrote himself *Porgy and Bess.*
There's a new young cat, concert player, Andre Watts, darker 'n
me, plays Brahms and Chopin like their breath is inside him."

I was unpersuaded and would make many pilgrimages in the
coming years to the ghetto clubs and after-hours joints (where
passing remarks dropped on an ofay could be coolly withering and
edged with menace: *You from somewhere else and lost your way,*
Jim, or just slummin'?...Hey, lemme ast you somethin'—the
buckles on the shoes means you're queer, right?), tracking the
elusive secret, searching out the passion and sensibility of the
black man. Hoping for a miracle of transmutation.

My first stop: the New World, north of 110th Street.

Harlem was beginning to put on a hostile face for the
Caucasian *turistas.* The years when affluent whites could pass a
flavorful evening slumming in the district's cafés and restaurants
were nearing an end. Making the rounds of the celebrated places
I'd read of and been told about—Savoy Ballroom, Small's Paradise,
Apollo Theater, Royal Roost, and Minton's Playhouse with its
faded awning and dingy wall mirrors, where the musical rebellion
had ignited in the early Forties—I was an easy target for frisky
young Harlem bloods, easy to pick out for reasons beyond my
whiteness.

"Look how slick this boy looks in his green sky. That chapeau
come from Switzerland, right?" (I was nineteen and affecting a
spruce kelly-green alpine hat.)

"I guess, Originally...,

"What you call a mountain hat."

"Alpine, yes."

"Now what might a elegant lid like that be worth would you say in the current market?"

"Stop cappin' on the boy, Clarence, he' s just around to hear the sounds."

"Well now, if he wants to dwell in our sunshine he got to come out of the shade. . . ."

A half-formed sense of vulnerability told me it was time to cut out.

"The hat came out of a trash bin. I doubt you could get four bits for it. See you guys. . ." I waved off amicably and headed across the street—solemn dark faces keeping vigil above me, gazing down from lighted brick-framed windows—to the storefront café from which music crackled and charged through the open door into the mild evening like a snarl of high-tension wires.

What I heard inside was something fierce, uncompromising and beautiful, an abrasive fiery sound that ran roughshod through all previously decreed rhythmic and harmonic structures. Here were the fabled "cutting sessions" I'd been told about—initiation rites which were in effect pitched battles, mostly black on black, for whites were still chary of joining the fray. Musicians spoke of "taking" one another, were scornful of outsiders and waited eagerly to ambush anyone who arrived with a burgeoning reputation. *Jump, chump, or I'll burn you up, you don't know nothin'.* After a few nights I began to understand that these sessions served as pressure cookers in which one earned recognition and esteem. Reputations could be made, reinforced or savaged in the course of one scorching set, and amateurs and

imposters got weeded out in a hurry; in the annealing process the music tightened up, grew leaner, more sublime.

I asked about the policy of sitting in and was told, anyone can, but you better be able to fly real good or they'll shoot you down, burn you up. And watching night after night in the close-packed, churning clubs I saw how awesome the firepower was onstage, how efficiently those without strong wings were cut down. These were schooled, confident, nerveless musicians who had found within themselves a core of calm enabling them to adjust to the roaring tempos and turbulent patterns, a cool and secret site from which to launch their blazing cascades of notes. They had done battle in a thousand sessions, knew their horns inside out and could not be fazed by key or tempo. Nor did they show any mercy, constantly raising the ante, calling unconventional tunes with swift-changing harmonies in strange keys at tempos so blistering you either soared or went down in flames. I suffered in vicarious misery with a pianist who sat with his hands in his lap throughout a tune kicked off at a vicious tempo, then quietly rose and retreated with a foolish downcast smile and pitiful squaring of shoulders that was like an attempt to pull a tattered threadbare cloak of dignity about himself. That was it, you either measured up or slunk away. It didn't take me but a minute to realize I was nowhere near ready for this league; they were lying in wait for the likes of me. If you don't have the price of admission, stay out of the hall. I began to suspect that the skills required for entry—so deeply ingrained in the Negro experience of despair, anger and struggle—might lie forever beyond my reach.

Chastened, I returned to Boston, where I was studying at the Berklee College of Music while supporting myself playing occa-

sional gigs with Rudy Yellin's Society Orchestra, and continued my search in the black after-hours clubs of eastern Massachusetts; here the music would be less convulsive and searing, the animus more manageable.

For a young white traversing the urban ghettos during the Fifties a horn case was often a talisman of safe passage.

"What you got in there, man?"

"Alto sax. On my way to a session."

"Oh? Where at?"

Possessing no such identifying badge and looking the way I did (a turnpike barmaid had once remarked behind my back, "The breath my seven-year-old uses to blow out her birthday candles would bowl him over"), I improvised: a sheaf of music manuscript paper under my arm, or an empty battered clarinet case I'd found discarded in a union-hall trash can. Often I came directly from a gig in my tux; this could prove an advantage—smoothing the rites of passage—or (more likely) a liability, depending on the character of the district I was passing through. I usually took the precaution of removing my bow tie and wearing a beat-up raincoat over the soup and fish.

Colleages at Berklee steered me to Coffee John's, an after-hours place on lower Massachusetts Avenue. The doors opened around ten, but the real action didn't get under way until after midnight when musicians began dropping by from work to drink and jam. A dingy narrow corridor of a room lined with scarred wooden booths facing a small cramped stage.

Guileless, fortified by an instinctive faith in my own inviolability and the holiness of my cause, I sauntered one night into a maelstrom of turbulent sound and close-together black faces,

white teeth, hands holding cups and glasses of coffee laced with
rye and gin; a low-pitched jumble of voices beneath the music's
pulse, the square patch of dance floor packed with weaving bodies.
For the better part of a week I hung out (when I told my white
friends where I'd been until four in the morning they blanched),
standing alone at the beer-and wine bar, which shut down by law
at one o'clock and was separated from the main room by a
shoulder-high partition, listening to the music and watching the
dancers, ignored but for an occasional curious or indifferent stare,
a half-frown etched in a questioning glance. On a Sunday night I
asked if I could sit in. The music was strong and gutty but within
my ken. I knew most most of the tunes; the tempos seemed
comfortable. I sensed that one or two of the pianists could play
rings around me, but the rings were concentric and not all that
wide. I felt I wouldn't be embarrassed as I would have been at the
incandescent Harlem sessions.

The trumpet player nominally in charge of the session nodded
(I learned later that many of the participating musicians were out
of work, that a handful of key players were paid a few dollars a
night for their midnight-to-four a.m. stints) and the pianist,
Lonnie, slid off the stool and leaned against a booth, hands in
pockets, his stony gaze sliding past my shoulder. I fiddled with the
stool's height, inadvertently lowering it, then spinning it up a few
revolutions, hearing mocking, skeptical voices behind me: "Already
I don't like the looks of this" and "What's this peckerwood gonna
do, tune it?" and "Come back, Lonnie, all's forgiven."

"'Blue Skies' okay?" the trumpet player said.

"Sure."

"One flat, you got four bars. 'Bout here," he said, snapping his thumb and middle finger in a lazy circle.

The rhythm falling in behind me was jagged and looser than it had sounded from the floor, looser than I was accustomed to— base and drums glancing off the beat, churning and slipping around it, rather than hammering it down four-square like spikes in a railbed. Several times I felt the meter sliding out from under my fingers. When this occurred the bass player steadied into a fundamental four-to-the-bar stroll, laying groundwork beneath me; at the same time I experienced the childhood sensation of being effortlessly lifted up on his shoulders (as an uncle had once hoisted me on a summer morning so I could see the parade unfolding down Worcester's main street). The dancers, I noticed uneasily, were drifting off the floor, some shaking their heads. "It don't get it," I heard someone say. I struggled through two more tunes, hands cramping and sweat dropping off my chin onto the keys until the board was slick as an ice rink. The dancers never returned.

The bass player, whose name was Lucius, a slim greying man with high cheekbones and a burgundy cast to his skin, took me aside after the set. "You want a honest critique?" he said and continued even as I nodded earnestly, mopping my face. "The dancers was off balance, that's why they deserted, they couldn't pat their feet right or make their proper moves. You was playing rhythmic enough, don't misapprehend me, but it was too straight-ahead and ricky-tick, if you catch my drift. We're used to a wider beat, space and margin to move around in. It's like a woman sashaying down a wide alleyway swinging her hips and buns, used

to plenty of leeway so's she won't bruise herself on the walls, you picture it? Now that alleyway suddenly *narrows* on her and this fine bitch is getting bruised, *hurting,* so naturally she' s going to cut out. What you got to do is listen to me and the iron and skins [drums] more intensely. . ."

I knew what he meant, sort of. Whether I could do anything about it was another matter. The twin legacies I had to overcome were my white upbringing and a two-year stretch playing businessman's-bounce show tunes, horas, and Viennese waltzes with a clam-and-chowder society band.

I don't kow why they kept letting me sit in; it must have taken guts, or simpleness, on my part to ask. Perhaps they were flattered by my interest in their music and derived satisfaction from the role reversal at a time when there were no black teachers in the public schools; or they may have found amusement in the spectacle of Master Charles getting turned on, picking their brains, trying to dwell in their sunshine—tolerant of me because I was just a skinny, earnest, funny-ass kid and not too obvious a nigger lover.

I became aware of a grudging cordiality as I poked my head in each night just after twelve bells. "Here comes the gopher in the watermelon patch" (Nestor, the bartender) and "Where's the sergeant-at-arms? Who let this white trash in?" As I made my way up to the stand a gruff, good-natured raillery followed me. "Better be wearin' your asbestos vest, boy. . . This paddy's gonna get his feathers clipped again. . . What's he gonna play for us tonight, 'Ol' Man Ribber' or 'Short'nin' Bread'?"

There was a beautiful tawny-skinned singer who occasionally sat in. She worked in a show bar on Columbus Avenue and would arrive after one-thirty in a luxurious leather coat, a silver tiara riding a towering knot of blue-black hair, eyes liquid and glittering with the night. Her name was Jonella; a chain smoker with a rich deep grainy voice (which was *why* she smoked, she insisted, to retain that *timbre*), she was always a little stoned, or seemed so to me, saying funny unconnected things, her luminous heavy-lidded eyes looking at you and sliding past you at the same time.

"Don't bust your conk, baby," she'd say to me, apropos of nothing, "everything's gonna be everything."

One night after I'd backed her for a set she introduced the musicians, inventing names she didn't know or remember ("On drums, in lavender trunks and green bathrobe, weighing in at one sixty-four and three-eighths, Rufus Funk, Jr."), and when it came my turn—"Let's give this slick boy on piano whose name I'll think of in a minute a hand for comin' across town and filling in so capably. He's all by his lonesome, innocent and taking care of business, so all you scroungy-ass chicks out there keep your hands off him, hear?" The crowd snickered and guffawed, enjoying the banter.

Off the stand, blowing plumes of smoke over my shoulder, she said, "You starting to get it, baby. You only got one main obstacle to surmount as I see it, which is that when I grew up tapping my feet and clapping my hands, singing 'Shadrach' and 'Swing Low Sweet Chariot' in my uncle's church you were singing 'Rock of Ages' and 'God Bless America.' But don't pay it too much mind," she advised, her liquid eyes gliding past me, "'cause one of these

days you're gonna score a touchdown and fifty thousand people'll be watching the game."

She had a cousin or half brother, Wesley—both were vague about the relationship—with the same distracted opaline gaze. Wesley washed cars during the day and came to Coffee John' s every night, sometimes sitting in on conga drum or beating a woodblock with a drumstick during Latin tunes. He spent a lot of time in the men's room, and when he wasn't there or on the stand he flitted genially up and down the line of booths, stopping to chat and sample a spiked coffee. In regard to me, he gave generously of his counsel.

"What this boy should do is spend some nights at the Arcady Lounge over on Huntington, observe how those ace bitches synchronizes their hips and butts to the drummer's accents— that's where he'll learn to swing."

"Now what would you know about swing, Wesley?" someone chimed in disdainfully. "You couldn't swing a Mickey Mouse watch on a rubber band."

"I'm sayin' the ec-*dysiasts* is where it's at—those righteous ebon girls wriggling their saucy dusters!" Wesley exclaimed, eyes widening and gleaming in opalescent splendor. "Couple nights at the Arcady that beat'll begin to sink in like a pile driver. Can't help but happen!"

The next time I saw him he'd forgotten the ecdysiasts; New York City was where I should go to pursue my education. "If the boy's serious in his endeavor"—the discussions seemed always to be directed past or lobbed over me, as if my presence were an obstacle to be circumvented—"he's got to earn his credits. The

only place to pick up that final diploma is the University of the Streets of New York."

"The Apple is cool," someone else observed somberly, "but rotten at the co'."

"I've already been," I said. "It's rough."

"It's where you got to go to pick up the pearls," Wesley continued, unheeding.

"You got to slog through some heavy mud to get to them pearls," the other said, dubious.

"There's nothin' new, man," a third interjected. "There's nothin' *new!* You don't have to set foot off your back porch. Just hang out, pick up an' get nervous like the rest of us."

"In that town," Wesley said with a touch of awe in his voice, "without the proper credits you can't even cross 125th Street, never mind Fifth Avenue."

I no longer felt the need to carry manuscript paper or an empty clarinet case with me, and had ceased standing alone at the bar; in the crowded cozy booths my jug became communal, alternating with the pints and half pints of my colleagues. On the bruised upright (that was treated lovingly, tuned once a month) I was starting to get it, at least some nights I thought I was (*It* is as hard to define as pornography, but I know it when I hear it), assimilating the displaced, driving rhythms and crackling improvisational patterns, sharpening my ear and expanding my repertoire. My fondest dream was that the Coffee John's regulars would one night rise en masse as I came off the stand, shouting, "The blue-eyed devil plays black!" From Lucius and Everett, a massive older pianist with a wild tangle of snow-flecked hair and a

rollicking bravura stride style reminiscent of Fats Waller's, I was discovering what "time" meant—the *quality* of the beat, just as timbre is the quality of the tone—and learning to function at very fast and very slow tempos. At slow tempos the beat has to *swell*, Lucius told me, and passed on the concept of his friend, the fiery west-coast pianist, Hampton Hawes: "It's like taking yourself a mouthful of good wine, swishing it around, savoring it before you let it go down; the swallow is that beat finally dropping." On up-tempos Everett showed me how to stay loose and relaxed by visualizing myself riding a train "rocketing along at a good clip, ninety miles an hour or more, but it doesn't trouble you 'cause you're sitting there cool and collected, your body swaying and rocking naturally with the train's pulse, which is the drums and bass. You don't need to be stomping your feet and getting all cramped up and over-excited." He suggested I listen to some old piano-roll rags and gave me a list of recordings. "That's where everything comes out of. Get that feeling down and it'll open an alley up the middle of your style wide enough for a moose to swing in. Inside the same eight bars there's sass, there's ecstasy, there's heartbreak. And listen to the Iowa boy, Beiderbecke, the cornet on 'I'm Comin' Virginia.' Same thing." (I listened. Bix's horn, rising from a morass of tubas, banjos and trap drums, rang like a carillon in the mountains, lonely, sorrowful and piercing. And those old rags that made my scalp tingle and triggered a grainy current down my backbone—what was there in them, even the jaunty ones, that left such a residue of sadness and ache?)

But the supreme lesson I was beginning to absorb—and it's an abstract and elusive one—is that *time* should be as "natural as a heartbeat pumping pure fresh blood into a tune."

There were occasional nights when the clientele turned over or out-of-town musicians dropped by, and the attitude toward me could change as swiftly as the sky on a March day. As soon as I walked in I could feel, like a radio's hum before the sound begins, a tension rise in the room, the friendly or incurious looks of the previous weeks suddenly vigilant and somber. When I sat in a standard tune would be called in a strange key at a murderous tempo—much faster than the regulars would ever kick it off. An unmistakable chill, unsheathed daggers on the stand. I couldn't help but remember what had befallen musicians with suspect credentials at the ferocious Harlem sessions, where the take-charge players had showed no mercy, ambushing newcomers and forcing them to retire in disgrace. I floundered badly through a headlong "Perdido"—the conclusion greeted out front by embarrassed silence, broken by an angry voice I recognized as Jonella's. "Raise off the boy, biggie, you don't need to show all those feathers." The intent was plain: Master Charles lured into the deep end of the pool before being blown out of the water.

If you didn't bring your cleats, stay off the field.

Jonella slipped an arm around my shoulder as I came off the stand, sweat-soaked and confused. "Don't pay those uppity dudes any mind, baby. They'll be pickin' trash out of the gutter while you're riding the elephant down the main street, just wait 'n' see. Everything's gonna be everything."

It was a sobering reminder that despite the previous air of geniality and counsel, the barrier was still there and always would be—made up of divergent experiences, temperament, attitudes—a skin-thin membrane but tough and impervious as sheet metal.

Gun-shy, licking my wounds, I stayed off the stand for a few nights. Then, with no sign of the marauders' return, I wandered gingerly back, testing the water. On a Friday, a week after my humbling, I had a good night, winning accolades for my solos, and only Jonella's absence prevented my sense of triumph and renewed self-esteem from being complete. When she came in a little later, I said, "I scored a touchdown, baby, you didn't even see the game."

She regarded me in her glancing sidelong way. "You're not only beginning to play colored, you're talkin' colored."

"Well, you right."

Her look turned reproachful. "Now don't you go cappin' on me with that nigger talk. You be respectful."

"Jonella, listen, I respect you more than anyone I know."

Something cunning infiltrated her expression. The tapering face with its yellowish-mauve tinge, glistening red mouth and luminous eyes was like an exotic African flower, and my heart slammed in my throat. She grinned at me then—an audacious, violent smile—gave her shoulders a brief wild shake and pivoting regally in her satin dress and spike heels, sashayed away down the line of booths.

She didn't seem to belong to anyone. She usually arrived alone and left alone—unless it was with her cousin (or half brother) Wesley—and was no longer working at the Columbus Avenue show bar; I had dropped by to see her early one night and found the place shuttered. Lacking the courage of my infatuation I never asked to see her home, wherever it was. There was no way I was going to leave the club with her; not in 1952 on the outskirts of

Dorchester at four in the morning weighing 130 pounds in a winter overcoat.

But she was right, the rhythms and idioms of the black culture were permeating my speech patterns as well as the texture of my playing. "Ain't that a bitch," I might say, registering surprise, wonder or delight. I no longer departed, I "cut out." "A nickel" was five dollars, and "a dime" ten. I wore a "sky" or "lid," not a hat. Someone trying to get my attention was "pulling my coat," and a musician playing strong and confidently with an element of grandstanding was "showing feathers" or "fluffing out his feathers"; if I were greatly impressed by his performance I "wigged." With reference to women, "ace broad" or "fine bitch" were expressions of the highest approbation, but Charles had better be careful in what context and with what inflection he flaunted the argot.

One night I had my first taste of pot. ("Tea," "Mary Jane," and "shit" were the prevailing expressions then.) I don't know how I'd avoided it for so long—except that its use was nowhere near as universal as it would become a decade later. I knew Wesley and others were lighting up in the john—I had been present once or twice when a joint was being passed around—and this night, by whim, or an accident of timing, I was included. "Try some of this Panama Red," Wesley said casually as the joint came back to him from a youth in a tattersall vest. I'd wondered off and on about the sensation and saw no reason not to indulge; it would be a sociable gesture as well as a new experience, akin to accepting a passed-around jug in the booths and taking a pull without wiping the neck. "It's truly evil shit, senor," Tattersall Vest said in a choked

voice. I had watched enough musicians smoke to know what to do. The joint had a rich powerful aroma, a piney fragrance. I took several deep pulls, holding the smoke in my lungs as long as I could. When I left the toilet I felt a languorous buzz in one ear as if a somnolent and not particularly bothersome fly had lodged there; and moments later an airy drifting lightness as if my brain had come unmoored and were floating gravity-free around my skull like flakes in a paperweight globe. Well, I thought leisurely, this shit is a gas. I don't know how long I stood by the stage listening to the music, all soft peaks and hollows, watching through a trembling blue smoke haze the congenial clusters of Coffee John's regulars, brothers all (ace boon coons), smoking and jiving and sipping their spiked coffee. Lucius was beckoning me back to the stand. Grinning loosely, confidently (someone told me later), I spun the vacated stool up and up—for some reason it was imperative that I assume a commanding position over the board; it took a long time to reach its summit. The trumpet player, Hardy, called "Black and Blue" and began snapping his fingers in a soft staccato crack, his hand tracing blurred ovals before my eyes. I played a four-bar intro, notes slipping effortlessly off my fingers (long-stemmed flowers trailing from a crystal vase). Innumerable languid choruses drifted by, brass and reeds soloing. Someone poked me in the back: my turn. I broke out and away (a limber colt), chords stacking neatly beneath my left hand like rubber coits, the right hand fleet, darting, venturous. After what seemed a half dozen choruses I reined in (not wanting to show too many feathers), looking around for one of the horns to reenter. "Keep goin'," Hardy said. "Enough, six choruses, don't wanna hog," I told

him. Hardy was smiling down at me in a puzzled, half-frowning way. "You ain't even reached the bridge of your first yet."

I remember little else of the evening, only of sauntering down the long corridor of booths—the gritty linoleum floor oddly soft and yielding as if I were walking on blankets or cork—a close-up gallery of faces gleaming at me like dark ivory through the sifting lavender smoke. I seemed to be taking a sinuous path, wandering unwillingly from booth to booth, my shoulders thumping against the wooden supports; it was like promenading the deck of a rolling ship without the accompanying sensation of vertigo. As I lurched for the door someone opened it for me, then someone else was hugging me, someone who smelled like a whole backyard of gardenias; a warm, faintly disappointing embrace, though, one of fraternity rather than romance. "Baby, you feelin' awright?"

"I'm cool," I told Jonella. "Everything's everythin'."

"Had hisself some o' Wesley's Panama Red," a disembodied voice said as the throbbing pumping music propelled me out the door like a giant hand pushing at my back.

I recall getting in my car and a wall of honking horns behind me, then rolling weightlessly from window to window in the deep swaying back seat of a taxi. I woke at 2:30 the next afternoon in my room on Fairfield Street feeling unanchored, my extremities—fingers, toes, ears—numb and tingling as if I'd been out on a freezing day underdressed and was just beginning to thaw. I drank something cold and metallic-tasting from a juice jar in the refrigerator, dressed and caught a bus to Massachusetts Avenue to look for my Studebaker. It took me an hour and a half, starting at Coffee John's and roaming in widening concentric circles, under

sober observation from upper-story windows, the framed faces as fixed, doleful and expressionless as those in old sepia photographs. The car was parked five blocks west of the club. The right rear wheel was up on the curb and the headlights were burning; a ticket under the wiper flapped in a gusting wind. The key was still in the ignition. I got in, shut off the lights and tried to start the motor, noticing two youths watching from the opposite curb. It whirred thinly, coughed, tubercular...faded. I waited a half minute and tried again: a feeble complaint, another quiet cough, and she died like a dog. The two observers were crossing the street toward me, one tall and slim with a thin fuzz of mustache, wearing a poplin jacket; the other was much smaller and lighter-skinned, a plumpish baby face tucked in the hood of a bulky gray sweat shirt. I rolled down the window and asked where the nearest gas station was.

"Got yourself some trouble, huh?" the tall youth said. "Why don't we take us a peek under the hood."

Maybe like Wesley he worked with cars; black kids, I thought, seemed to know a lot about cars. I got out and lifted the hood, propping it on its stick.

The two silently inclined their heads, inspecting the innards. "Hard to say," the tall boy said after a moment.

"Where's the nearest station?" I asked again.

"Oh, there's nothing for a ways around here," the tall boy said. He stuck his hands in his poplin jacket, regarding me in an unhurried thoughtful manner.

"We could use money for ciggies," the other said in a piping voice that matched his face, the light brown eyes limpid, vacuous, trusting, hands folded into the gray pouch of his sweat shirt.

"I...didn't bring my wallet," I said truthfully, shivering a little though it wasn't that cold, wishing I had brought my empty clarinet case for show.

"Any kind of change will do," the tall boy said reasonably.

"I only brought bus fare, some quarters..." I fumbled in my pants pocket.

"That'll get it," the tall boy said, holding out a soft palm as pink as a frosted wafer.

I looked around me, at the afternoon shadows darkening the brick buildings, the sun hanging wan and thin, a pale disc pasted on the rim of the November sky; a gust of wind blew dry papers along the gutter. I played the coins carefully into the pink palm. "I'm a musician," I blurted and knew immediately it was a mistake.

"Oh?" The tall boy pocketed the change. "Where at do you play?"

"Coffee John's. Actually I just sit in nights whenever—"

"Where's that at?" The tall youth's eyes had rolled leisurely upward and away, the mouth compressed and rubbery.

"Over on Mass. Avenue, maybe five blocks—"

"What d'you play?" the small boy asked, respectful.

"Piano," I said, which was my second mistake.

The small boy brought something out of the pouch of his sweat shirt, pressed a thumb to it—there was a faint whirring sound— and drew it carefully along the back of my right hand; I thought I heard a soft tearing, like tissue paper parting. Both youths were racing down the street then, yards apart; the small plump boy surprisingly swift, outdistancing the other. The surrounding buildings were now completely in shadow and a piercing chill had fallen over the street. With a sigh I dropped my eyes. There was a

thin red line across the knuckles, the skin parted delicately like paper. I reclined against the fender of the car, watching the blood suddenly bloom, incredibly bright, bubbling and winking like a ruby chain in artificial light.

The wind had risen; it had grown colder. I was glancing listlessly toward both intersections and around at the silent, darkening buildings, wondering which way to turn or go, or whether to go anywhere at all, when a car stopped in the middle of the street. "What's up, man, what's the problem?"

It was Wesley, poking his head out the window of a faded green Chevy, the whites of his eyes flaring as they fixed on the bloodsoaked handkerchief. Everett was in the passenger seat beside him. They pulled over to the curb and got out.

Everett took my hand in his and gently peeled back the clotted cloth; I felt nothing.

Wesley's breath expelled as if he'd been punched in the chest. "Oh, man, who did you like that?"

"Couple kids. I thought they were going to help..." I motioned my head vaguely in the direction they had fled.

"You jus' never knows any more, all these weirdies cruisin' the avenues. Why jus' last week I was over Huntington comin' out of—"

"Stop the damn jabbering and let's *go*," Everett said, "we got to get this nigger to a doctor."

Riding between them, my legs cushioned by Everett's massive thighs—a fat man's inadvertent caress—a tangle of emotions swept in on me. Bewilderment and wonder that the locus of the music that was my breath and heartbeat should also be the source

of animosity and venom. It would take courage to venture to this part of town again; the barrier had been raised a notch, made more forbidding, fortified with steel...But even as the pain took hold of my hand with the car's jounce and rattle, my spirits began to lift, a small glow of assurance warmed me as Everett's words echoed far back in my mind...*Let's go, we got to get this nigger to a doctor.* Within the urgency, the humorous play and idiom, was a suggestion of alliance, kinship, acceptance: I had made it a little way through the barrier.

I turned to Wesley. "That was some powerful Panama Red last night."

Wesley nodded solemnly. "I can dig it."

*

A thin white scar remains, riding the ridge of the knuckles like a badge of initiation, an emblem of battle.

I never scored the big touchdown, never made it all the way through to the other side—none of us whiteys do—but ten years later, when I was house pianist at the *hungry i* in San Francisco, a middle-aged black man approached me in the bar following an entr'acte medley of Duke Ellington tunes. He said he had enjoyed the music and that I must have grown up or spent a lot of time around Harlem to play like that. I told him I had been born and bred in eastern Massachusetts. "Okay," he said, "but somewhere along the line you must've eaten some okra and sweet potato pie."